D0088558

Peggy Parish

HERMIT DAN

Illustrated by
Paul Frame

A YEARLING BOOK

Published by
Dell Publishing Co., Inc.,
1 Dag Hammarskjold Plaza
New York, New York 10017

Yearling ® TM 913705, Dell Publishing Co., Inc.

ISBN: 0-440-43501-3

Reprinted by arrangement with Macmillan Publishing Co., Inc.
Printed in the United States of America
Second Dell printing—June 1981
CW

For Guri Lowrie,
my young Norwegian friend,
with love

Contents

1. Robertses' House
2. Robertses' Inlet
3. Hermit Dan's Garden
4. Grandpa's Stream
5. The Cave
6. Widow Hawkins's
7. Hermit Dan's Shack
8. Summer People's Area

PIRATE ISLAND

N

S

1

An Early
Birthday

"Is it time yet?" asked Liza.

"It's two minutes closer than when you asked me last," said Grandpa.

"A minute sure can be long," said Bill.

"Especially when you're waiting for something special," said Jed.

"And electric lanterns are really special," said Bill. "Gee, Grandpa, what gave you and Gran the idea of giving us early birthday presents?"

"Oh, Gran and I talked it over and we decided with all the exploring you do, the lanterns would come in handy," said Grandpa. "No point in waiting until your birthdays when you needed them now."

"And we do need them," said Jed. "I want to explore that cave we found."

"Is that the only cave you're interested in?" asked Grandpa.

The children looked at him in surprise.

"What do you mean?" asked Bill. "Isn't that the only cave?"

"Nope," said Grandpa. "Didn't your father tell you about his cave?"

"His cave!" said the children.

"He was the first Roberts we know of to find it," said Grandpa. "I'm surprised he didn't tell you about it."

"I guess when you told him not to tell your stories, he thought you meant that one, too," said Jed.

"Where is it? Tell us about it!" said Bill.

"Is it as big as the other one?" asked Liza.

"Hold it!" said Grandpa. "One at a time. I'm not going to tell you where it is. That would take the fun out of your finding it. And no, Liza, it's not quite as big as the other cave."

"How did Dad find it?" asked Jed.

"By accident," said Grandpa. "He was sure this island was once a pirates' hiding place. When he found the cave we knew about, he was even more convinced. He searched the island from one end to the other looking for proof."

"You know something, Grandpa?" said Jed. "I believe that, too."

"Oh, oh," said Bill. "Here we go. I can feel it right down to my toes."

"Yep," said Liza. "Me, too."

2

"Feel what?" asked Grandpa.

"That we're going to look for proof that pirates were here," said Bill.

"We just get one mystery solved and up pops another," said Liza. "I can tell it by the look in Jed's eyes."

"Well, you don't have to help," said Jed grumpily.

"Just try and leave us out," said Liza. "Could you have solved Grandpa's mystery without us?"

"No," said Jed. "I'm sorry. I didn't mean to be grumpy. We're a team."

"And a team sticks together," said Bill. He patted Jed on the back.

"Besides, I'm getting bored," said Liza. "It's fun to swim and all, but . . . ."

"I know what you mean, Liza," interrupted Bill. "We want action."

Liza, Bill and Jed were spending the summer with their grandparents on Pirate Island. The Robertses had owned a home there for several generations, but this was the children's first visit. Their grandparents usually came for the month of December when the caretaker and his wife were away. But the caretaker had died and his wife had gone to live with her daughter. So Gran and Grandpa had decided to spend the summer, and they had invited Liza, Bill and Jed to stay with them.

Many years before, when Grandpa was just a boy, his older brother had made up a treasure hunt for Grandpa and his sister. He had hidden some things belonging to different members of the family on the island. He planned to have them find the treasure the following summer. But things had not worked out as he planned. It was many years before the family returned to the island. The brother left home to go to work. Before he left, he gave them the first clue. But later he was killed in an accident. The treasure hunt had never taken place.

Just before coming to the island, Grandpa had told the children the story and given them the first clue. As soon as they got to the island, Liza, Bill and Jed had set out to find the treasure. It was a hard puzzle, but they finally had solved it. Now they were ready for a new adventure.

"Well, you can go into action now," said Grandpa. "It's just about time for the boat."

"Hooray!" shouted the children.

"Let's go," said Bill.

"Hold it a minute," said Gran. The children turned. They had not heard her come out.

"What's wrong?" asked Jed.

"Nothing's wrong," said Gran. "But there's a grocery order as well as your package coming on that boat. So please take the wagon—that is, if you want to eat."

"Right away, Mam," said Bill. "Eat is something I always want to do."

He ran to get the wagon.

There were no stores on Pirate Island. People called in their orders to Mainland and the supplies were delivered by motorboat. One end of the island was a summer resort,

4

and during the vacation season the boats ran several times a day. At other times the boats came only a couple of times a week as only a few people lived on the island all year round and some of them had their own boats.

"Okay," said Bill. "Here I am, wagon and all. Let's go."

The children started for the dock.

"I'm so excited," said Liza. "It feels like it's really my birthday."

"Then that would make it mine, too, twin sister," said Bill.

"It still wouldn't make it mine," said Jed, "but who cares as long as we get the lanterns."

"But it's going to seem funny when our birthdays do come and no presents from Gran and Grandpa," said Liza.

"Want to bet?" said Bill.

"What do you mean?" asked Liza.

"You know how Gran and Grandpa have always been," said Bill. "When it's our birthday they always send Jed a present, too. Then when it's his birthday, they send us presents."

"Bill's probably right," said Jed. "I think this is Gran and Grandpa's way of getting around Mom and Dad's rule about not spoiling us."

"Hurry," said Liza. "The boat is pulling in."

The children ran. They got to the dock just as the men began to unload the boat.

5

"Hello there," called a boatman. "We have a big package for you. It just made the boat."

"Thank goodness," said Bill. "We really need that package."

"Be careful," said the man. "It's marked Fragile."

Jed took the package. The children started for home. Then Liza said, "I can't wait."

The boys looked at each other. Bill took the package and quickly tore it open. Three shining electric lanterns were unwrapped.

"Wow!" said Bill. "Look at how big they are."

"They sure beat flashlights," said Jed. "Now we can really explore."

"Did they send the batteries?" asked Liza. Jed dug around in the package.

"Yep," he said. "Here they are."

Quickly they put the batteries in the lanterns.

"Now that's what I call good light," said Bill. "Come on, let's go show Gran and Grandpa."

Suddenly Liza stopped. She said, "The groceries!"

"Ye gad," said Bill. "Gran would skin us alive if we forgot them."

"I'll do it," said Jed. He ran back.

"Forgot a few things, didn't you?" said a boatman. "I tried to call you."

"I'm just glad Liza remembered," said Jed. "Gran would have had our heads."

The men laughed.

"Now," said Jed, "it's safe to go home."

When they neared the house, Liza shouted, "Gran, Grandpa! Look."

"What took you so long?" asked Grandpa. "I thought you would be right back."

The children looked at each other. They didn't know quite what to say. Bill started, "We stopped to open the package and—"

"I know," said Gran. "You forgot the groceries."

Everybody laughed.

2

Excitement Begins

"Say, Gran," said Bill, "could we have a picnic lunch and go exploring?"

"I knew you were going to say that," said Gran. "Your lunches are already made."

"One more question, Grandpa," said Jed. "Is the other cave close to your cave?"

"It would have to be," said Grandpa. "That end of the island isn't too wide. But you'll have to look carefully. I stopped by yesterday. The entrance is almost covered with bushes."

"Grandpa," said Liza, "did Dad have an electric lantern when he was a boy?"

"No," said Grandpa. "He used a kerosene lamp."

"Grandpa," started Bill.

"That's it," said Grandpa. "Off with you. Next thing

you will be wanting me to tell you exactly where the cave is."

The children laughed. Bill said, "Well, it was worth a try, anyway."

"Jed," said Gran, "do you have your watch?"

"I sure do," said Jed. "Why?"

"I want you children to be back by five o'clock," said Gran.

"Any particular reason?" asked Liza.

"Yes," said Gran. Then she saw Grandpa frowning and shaking his head. "I need you for something then."

"We'll be here," said Jed.

"Give them a little leeway," said Grandpa. "You never know what kind of things they might run into."

"That's true," said Gran. "Make it between five and five-thirty."

"That we'll do," said Bill. "Now let's go."

The children got their lunches and started out.

"What do you suppose that was all about?" asked Liza.

"I don't know," said Jed, "but something is up."

"Where shall we start?" asked Bill.

"At the big cave, I suppose," said Jed. "It's in about the center of the island and Grandpa said Dad's cave was nearby."

"We can leave our lunches there and spread out in both directions," said Liza. "We'll show Grandpa how quickly we can find that cave."

"I wonder what Grandpa meant when he said you never could tell what kinds of things we might run into?" asked Bill.

"Oh, you know," said Liza, "skunks and the usual things that seem to happen to us."

"Wouldn't it be great if we could find proof that pirates really were here?" said Jed.

"Don't get your hopes up too high, big brother," said Bill.

"I don't see why not," said Liza. "Nobody has proven they weren't here."

"Good point, Liza," said Jed. "And we don't give up easily."

"Not with you around, anyway," said Bill.

The children came to a branch in the path. One branch led to Grandpa's fishing spot. The other branch led to Hermit Dan's garden. Hermit Dan wasn't an honest-to-goodness hermit, but everybody called him that because he had very little to do with people and seemed to dislike children especially. Liza, Bill and Jed were afraid of him. But he was a good man and kept the islanders supplied with fresh vegetables. He never just gave them to the people, but left them by their doors. And he did not like to be thanked. Even though the children were afraid of Hermit Dan, they were also very curious about him.

"You know what?" said Liza.

"That's a dumb question," said Bill. "Of course we know 'what.' That's a first-grade word."

"And that's a dumb answer," said Liza. "You know what I meant."

"Okay," said Bill. "Tell us what."

"I would like to sneak by and get a good look at Hermit Dan's garden," said Liza.

"What!" said both boys.

"If he's there, you know what he'll do," said Jed.

"Yeah," said Bill. "We'd never find Dad's cave. We'd get the pounding of our lives with that stick he carries."

"I don't mean if he's there," said Liza. "But you know he usually works early in the morning. I just want to see it."

"I would kind of like to see it myself," said Jed.

"Then let's take a chance," said Bill.

"But remember, easy does it," said Jed. "Be just as quiet as you can."

"You don't have to say that twice," said Bill. "Remember, I've already felt that stick once."

The children sneaked through the bushes until they could see the garden.

"Hey," said Bill, "we're in luck."

"Hooray," said Liza. The children burst out of the bushes.

"Take a look at that," said Jed. "Not a weed in sight."

"Look at those raspberries!" said Liza. "They are my favorite fruit. Do you think he would notice if we pick some?"

"I don't know," said Jed. "I don't think I'd try."

"I can't see why not," said Bill. "After all, this is Grandpa's land. Come on, Liza."

Hermit Dan had built a fence around and over the garden to keep the wild animals out. Liza opened the gate, and the children went straight to the raspberry bushes. Liza popped a fat berry into her mouth. Then they heard a roar.

"Get out of my garden, you brats!" There stood Hermit Dan with two pails of water.

"We're sorry, sir," said Jed.

"It was just so pretty," said Liza. "And I couldn't resist those raspberries."

"I'm not sorry," said Bill. "This is our grandfather's land. We have a right to be here if we want to."

"You don't see your grandfather here working, do you?" said Hermit Dan. "He gave me permission to use this land. Now get out and don't come poking around here again." He picked up his stick and started waving it. He shouted, "Meddling brats!"

The children ran. They got out of the garden and out of sight quickly. Bill was still angry.

"You got us into this, Liza," he said. "You and your big ideas."

12

"I didn't hear you objecting," said Liza. "You didn't have to go."

"Oh, shut up, you two," said Jed. "We're all to blame. Now let's get on with finding that cave."

"He's just a mean old man," said Bill. "He had no right to scream at us that way."

"So forget about him," said Jed. "I'll race you to the cave."

3
Unexpected Events

"I won!" shouted Liza.

"That's because you took a head start," said Bill. "It doesn't count."

"I did not," said Liza. "And it does too count."

"Are you going to squabble all day," said Jed, "or do we get on with our plans?"

Before Bill or Liza had time to answer, they heard a loud, excited yapping.

"Jelly Bean!" said the children.

"I thought we left him inside," said Bill.

"We did," said Liza. "I guess Gran or Grandpa let him out."

"We better see what he's up to," said Jed.

"If he's found another skunk, let's just lose him," said Bill. "I can't go through all of that again."

"It sounds as if he's up by the spring," said Liza.

"Walk quietly," said Jed. "It might very well be a skunk. Jelly Bean never seems to learn."

The children went quietly, but quickly. It wasn't long before they saw the little black dog yapping his head off. The children couldn't help laughing. Jelly Bean was yapping and prancing around at the same time.

"What on earth is he after now?" said Liza.

"Well, it's not a skunk," said Bill. "A skunk would never let him get that close."

Suddenly Jelly Bean lay down. He peered into a hole in an old tree. Three curious children slipped up behind him. Jed picked Jelly Bean up. Jelly Bean yapped in protest. Quickly they looked in the hole.

"Baby rabbits!" said Bill.

"Oh, aren't they dear," said Liza. "Do you think I could hold one?"

"They look scared to death," said Jed.

"Wouldn't you be with all Jelly Bean's yapping?" asked Bill. Jelly Bean started yapping again as if to answer.

"I wonder where their mother is," said Bill. "I thought animal mothers fought for their babies."

"Jelly Bean probably scared her away," said Jed.

"Maybe she got killed or something," said Bill.

"Do let's take them home," said Liza. "I'm sure Gran and Grandpa would let us keep them."

"Let those rabbits be," said a gruff voice. The children turned in surprise. There stood Hermit Dan. The children were afraid to say anything.

16

"Don't you know anything about wildlife?" he asked. "You can't raise wild rabbits without their mother. The whole lot of them would be dead in a day or so."

"No, sir," said Jed. "We didn't know."

"Your grandfather needs to tell you a few things. At the rate you're going, you'll wreck this end of the island," said Hermit Dan. "Now stay away from those rabbits. They need their mother, not a yapping mongrel and yowling brats."

Hermit Dan turned and walked away.

"Wow," said Bill. "All he has to do is open his mouth and he scares me."

"At least he didn't have that stick," said Jed. "He might have killed us."

Liza was pale, and very quiet.

"But you know," said Jed, "he's right. We don't know that much about wildlife. We'd better talk to Grandpa."

"Why does he have to be so grumpy?" asked Bill. "I don't like being called a brat."

"Maybe underneath he's not so grumpy," said Liza. "Think how we would have felt if the baby rabbits had died."

"You're right, Liza," said Jed. "He really cares. He's an old man and look how far he carries water for his garden."

"And all the nice things he does for the islanders," said Liza.

"Then why does he hate children?" asked Bill. "We haven't done anything to him."

"Except raid his garden and disturb his peace with our howling through the woods," said Jed.

"Are you trying to say we can't have any fun?" asked Bill. "This is Grandpa's property."

"I don't think that's what Jed means," said Liza. "We have to get Grandpa to tell us more."

"And try to stay out of Hermit Dan's way," said Jed.

"I'm with you on that last one," said Bill. "Say, I'm hungry. Where are our lanterns and lunches?"

"Oh, no!" said Jed. He put his hand on his head. "We left them by Hermit Dan's garden."

"Gol-ll-y," said Bill. "What do we do now?"

"We have a choice," said Jed. "We can go home and come back later, or we can try to get them."

"This day is going all wrong," said Bill.

"I'm the smallest," said Liza. "I know where we left them. They're by some bushes. I think I can get them without his knowing."

"Aren't you scared?" asked Bill.

"Yes," said Liza. "But not scared enough to spoil our whole day. Just hold on to Jelly Bean."

"Okay, Liza," said Jed. "You're a good sport. Be careful."

Liza was scared. She didn't think that Hermit Dan would really hurt her. Nevertheless, she went as quietly as she could. Soon she could see the garden and Hermit Dan. She stopped and looked. He was at the far end of the garden with a basket, picking raspberries.

18

Liza breathed a sigh of relief. In a flash she darted out, grabbed the lunches and the lanterns and was back in the bushes. She felt a little shaky as she hurried back to the boys.

"Success," she shouted.

"Hooray for Liza," yelled the boys.

"Now can we have lunch?" asked Bill. "I'm going to be too weak to eat it soon."

"That will be the day," said Jed. "Okay, let's eat."

"But don't we want to try the lanterns in the cave first?" asked Liza.

"Sure," said Bill. "We'll have lunch there."

Liza wasn't too sure about that. It was kind of scary in the cave. But she didn't say anything. With lanterns and lunch, they crawled into the cave.

"Hey," said Bill. "How about that! These lanterns are great."

"They sure are," said Liza. "The cave looks so different. It's not a bit scary. For goodness sake, open that lunch. I'm starved."

The boys laughed at the way she said it.

"And she talks about my stomach!" said Bill.

4

Exploration

"Gran really outdid herself on that lunch," said Jed.

"She sure did," said Bill. "I'm stuffed."

"What time is it, anyway?" asked Liza.

"One-thirty," said Jed.

"Gee," said Bill, "we better get busy."

"Has anybody seen Jelly Bean?" asked Jed.

"Yes," said Liza. "He ate part of my lunch. And now he's sleeping in that corner."

The boys looked. They saw a contented puppy curled up asleep.

"Should we just let him be?" asked Bill.

"Huh-uh," said Jed. "You know that puppy. He'll have us in trouble again in no time. Where we go, he's going."

Liza went over and scooped up Jelly Bean. Then the children left the cave.

"Now what is our strategy going to be?" asked Bill.

"I've been thinking about that," said Jed. "Grandpa practically told us the other cave wasn't far from this one."

Liza and Bill looked at Jed. He was the best thinker of the three.

"Do you have any ideas?" asked Bill.

"Just a hunch," said Jed. "Usually with this kind of cave there are branch caves. I was looking around in this one. Did you notice that hole in the far side?"

"No," said Liza. "But what difference does it make?"

"I have a feeling it is a small tunnel that leads to another cave."

Bill turned and scooted back into the cave. The other two followed him.

"Hey," yelled Bill. "There *is* a hole here."

"Let me see, too," said Liza. Bill moved over.

"It's a hole, all right," said Liza. "But not even Jelly Bean could get through it."

"Gosh, you're dumb," said Bill. "We know that, but it is an important clue."

"Clue to what?" asked Liza.

Bill threw up his hands and said, "I give up. Why couldn't I have had a brother for a twin?"

"Just hold it, Bill," said Jed. "Do you know what it is a clue to?"

Bill looked at Jed. He stammered around. "Well—." Then he stopped. His face got red. He said angrily, "No, but at least I know it's a clue."

"Then quit yelling at Liza," said Jed.

"All right, Mr. Know-It-All," yelled Bill. "You two can look at that stupid hole. I'm going out and find the cave."

"Go ahead," said Jed. "I was only going to explain about the hole. I found a book on caves in Grandpa's library last night. That's the only reason I know."

Bill stopped. He looked interested.

"Sorry, Liza," he said. "I guess I can be pretty dumb, too. Truce?"

"Truce," said Liza, and shook Bill's hand.

"Okay, educate us," said Bill. He and Liza sat down.

"According to that book," said Jed, "this kind of rock cave sometimes leads to a whole network of others."

"You mean we may discover a new cave?" asked Bill excitedly.

"Could be," said Jed. "Or we may find that this one leads to Dad's cave."

"How can we tell?" asked Liza. "There's no way we can get through that little opening."

"But a long stick could," said Jed. "We could find out if anything is there."

"We had better start looking for a stick," said Bill. He stood up.

"I don't think we would find one long enough just lying around," said Jed.

"Do we have to go all the way back to the house and get a hatchet?" asked Liza.

"Nope," said Jed. He lifted his shirt. Strapped around his waist were his Boy Scout hatchet and knife.

"Good planning," said Liza. "Proud to have you for a brother."

"He does come in right handy at times," said Bill. "Let's go chop us a tree."

"I know what!" said Liza. "Bamboo! You know where that patch of bamboo is? It would be easy to get a long pole that way."

"Two brains in the family!" said Bill. "Bamboo would be perfect. It's not heavy and we could probe around with it."

"Good thinking," said Jed. "Let's go."

The children ran to the bamboo patch. Jed cut the longest pole he could find and stripped it.

"I'll even offer to carry it back," said Bill.

"That's big of you," said Liza. "You just want to have the first turn at poking it through that hole."

Bill grinned at her. Quickly they returned to the cave. Jelly Bean seemed to know something exciting was happening. He followed at Liza's heels, yapping all the way.

"If you don't hush, Jelly Bean," said Liza, "I'm going to stuff you through that hole."

"That's not a bad idea," said Jed. "Then if there is a way out, Jelly Bean would be sure to find it."

"That stupid dog!" said Bill. "All he knows how to do is yap and get into trouble."

23

Liza picked up Jelly Bean. She said, "Don't worry. We're just teasing."

Bill started into the cave.

"Hey," he called, "we're going to have trouble. The pole is longer than the cave is wide."

"Doesn't matter," said Jed. "Bamboo will bend. We'll just ease it in."

The children worked together. Soon they had the end of the pole in the hole. They kept bending and pushing. The pole slid right in.

"There *is* another cave!" shouted Bill.

"It may be just a tunnel," said Jed. "Let's see if we can tell how wide it is."

The pole moved freely as they probed around.

"Yippee!" they shouted.

"I think we've made a real discovery!" said Jed.

"But what do we do now?" asked Bill. Nobody said anything. Then Liza said, "You know, that just might be Dad's cave."

Jed thought about this and said, "You may be right. In that case, the entrance should be on the other side of this one."

"I know what," said Bill. "I'll poke the pole straight through as far as I can. One of you go over to the other side. See if you can find an entrance."

"Come on, Liza," said Jed. "We'll both go."

"Okay," said Liza. They took their lanterns and left the cave.

"Let's just scramble over the top of this one," said Jed. "That should put us in about the right place."

Liza followed Jed. She said, "All I see are bushes."

"Look closely," said Jed. "Remember, Grandpa said the entrance would be almost covered with bushes."

"Hey, hurry up," shouted Bill.

Liza and Jed stopped. Bill's voice sounded hollow. But it also sounded close by.

"Yell again," shouted Jed. "I think we're close."

"Okay," shouted Bill.

"I see it, I see it!" screamed Liza. She started through the bushes. Jed was right behind her.

"I wish I had worn long pants," said Liza. "My legs are getting all scratched."

"Same here," said Jed. "Turn on your lantern before you go in."

"Don't worry," said Liza. "I'm not going into any cave without light."

Jed turned on his lantern also. The two started into the cave. Jed called, "Stop poking, Bill. We've found it."

"Come over the top of the cave," called Liza. "I'll stay at the entrance with my lantern."

"Wahoo," shouted Bill.

5

Big Discoveries

"Who put a red rag on that bush?" asked Bill.

"What red rag on what bush?" asked Liza.

"I didn't see any red rag," said Jed.

"Come outside," said Bill. "I'll show you."

They crawled out of the cave. Bill said, "Now I ask you, is that a red rag or not?"

Liza and Jed stared at the rag.

"I bow to you, brother," said Jed.

"It is indeed a red rag," said Liza with a curtsy.

"Hmm," said Bill. "Some detectives you are."

"But who could have tied it there?" asked Jed. The children thought about this.

"Grandpa!" said Liza.

"Why Grandpa?" asked Bill.

"Maybe because he wanted to help us," said Jed.

"Remember he said the entrance was hard to find because it was almost covered with bushes?"

"But that just doesn't sound like Grandpa," said Bill. "He knew if we didn't find it today we would keep on looking. That sort of spoils it."

"It shouldn't," said Jed. "We found the cave without seeing the red rag."

"I still think it was Grandpa," said Liza.

"You're probably right," said Jed. "Did you see how he frowned and shook his head when Gran told us what time to get home? He's up to something."

"And it's up to us to find out what," said Bill. "So stop yakking and let's get down to business."

Bill scrambled into the cave. Liza and Jed were right behind him.

"Looks about like the other one," said Bill. "Just a little smaller."

"Hey," called Jed. "Take a look at this."

Liza and Bill ran over to Jed. Jed said, "See?"

"Wow!" said Liza. "Pictures!"

"Maybe this was an Indian cave," said Bill. "Didn't they make pictures like this?"

"Or maybe cavemen were here!" said Liza. "Let me take a closer look."

Liza held her lantern up higher. She said, "It must have been Indians because it looks like a buffalo hunt. I don't think cave men had bows and arrows."

28

"Ah, come on," said Jed. "Dad or Grandpa would have told us anything that exciting. I expect Dad did that."

"But maybe they didn't see them," said Bill. "Remember, they only had kerosene lanterns."

"Bill's right," said Liza. "We probably wouldn't have seen them with our flashlights."

"That still doesn't tell us why Grandpa wanted to help us find the cave," said Jed.

"Keep on looking," said Liza. "We'll find it if it's here."

"Maybe Grandpa is playing a trick on us," said Bill. "He knows how much we love a mystery."

"Maybe so," said Liza. "But Grandpa has never done that before."

"Yap, yap, yap!"

"Jelly Bean!" said Bill. "I forgot about him."

"I'll see what's wrong," said Liza. She went to the cave entrance. Then she started laughing and said, "Come here, you've got to see this."

The boys went to the entrance. They started laughing, too. There was Jelly Bean sitting in the top of some bushes.

"I'll get him," said Jed.

"How did he manage that?" asked Liza.

"Must have thought he could jump over the bushes instead of coming through," said Bill. "You know he does get big ideas."

"And he's so little," said Liza.

"Okay, back to work," said Jed.

"And you stay put, Jelly Bean," said Liza.

"Hey, come here!" said Jed. "There's a map on this wall."

Liza and Bill rushed over.

"A map!" said Liza.

"A real map!" said Bill. "Maybe it's a pirate's map."

"But what does it mean?" asked Jed.

The children studied the map. Bill said, "It doesn't make any sense to me."

30

"Nor to me," said Liza. "Any ideas, Jed?"

"This is no pirate's map," said Jed laughing. "This is a Grandpa's map."

"How do you know?" asked Liza. Jed held up a finger. There was chalk on it.

"That Grandpa sure has been busy," said Bill. "Does the map mean anything now?"

"I think so," said Jed. "This X marks where we are now. Right?"

"Yes," said Bill, "I can see that."

"Okay," said Jed. "Look where the arrows go."

"Why, they go to the spring," said Liza.

"Yeah," said Bill. "And there's another X there. Let's go."

"We're with you," said Jed. Liza picked up Jelly Bean and they left the cave. Suddenly Jed stopped.

"What's wrong?" asked Bill.

"Does anybody have a pencil and paper?" asked Jed.

"What for?" asked Bill.

"We need to copy that map," said Jed. "We can't keep running back to the cave."

"I don't have either one," said Liza.

Bill searched his pockets and said, "Neither do I."

"We'll have to go back and really study that map, then," said Jed. They trooped back into the cave.

"We'll never remember all of this," said Liza. Without a word, she left the cave.

"What's wrong with her?" said Bill.

"No telling," said Jed. "But she'll be back."

He was right. In just a few minutes Liza rushed back in.

"How's this?" she asked. She held up a piece of white birch bark and a stick.

"I don't get it," said Bill. "How does that help?"

"Liza, you're really smart," said Jed. "Want me to sharpen that stick?"

"Yep," said Liza.

Bill still looked puzzled. He said, "What's smart about a piece of bark and a stick? Seems dumb to me."

"You'll see," said Jed. "Here, you draw it, Liza. Show Bill what brains are."

Liza grinned. She spread the bark on the floor. She took the sharpened stick and began to draw the map.

Bill watched. Then he said, "Wow, that's neat. How did you ever think of that?"

"Don't you remember that year we studied Indians?" asked Liza. "This was one of the things we read about."

"Nope," said Bill. "I was more interested in the war whoops." Suddenly he started dancing around the cave, letting out terrible whoops.

"Stop it!" said Liza. "You're putting my ears out."

"And you'll have Hermit Dan over here, too, with all that noise," said Jed. "Can't you ever be serious?"

"It's not easy," said Bill. "But I'll try."

The expression on his face made Liza and Jed burst

out laughing. Bill held it as long as he could, then he started laughing, too. "Okay," he said. "Back to work, Liza."

Liza soon had the map copied. She said, "I think I got everything on it."

6

The Search Begins

"Okay," said Bill. "Now let's really go."

They crawled out of the cave. Jed stopped and looked at the red rag on the bush. He shook his head and said, "I still don't know how we missed that."

"I guess we were just excited," said Liza.

"Pooh," said Bill. "It just took old sharp eyes to spot it."

"Wait a minute," said Jed. "I think there's something on it." He reached over and untied the rag. Something was written on it. The children read it together.

"Blue!" they said.

"What could that mean?" asked Jed. All three children were puzzled.

"Boy," said Bill. "The Robertses sure do know how to make puzzling puzzles."

Liza and Jed laughed. Jed said, "This is as bad as the

first clue we had when we found the key to the treasure."

"I wonder if we will do this kind of thing when we have our own children," said Liza.

"If we don't get on with this," said Bill, "our children might have to do it for us. Let's head for the spring."

The children started running. Jelly Bean was at their heels, yapping, all the way.

"Here's the spring," said Jed. "Now what?"

"A drink of water," said Bill. "That run made me thirsty."

"Me, too," said Liza. "Do hurry, Bill."

"I could use a drink myself," said Jed. "That is the best water."

"And the coldest," said Bill. Then he started drinking again.

"Oh, come on, Bill," said Liza. "That's enough."

"Not for me," said Bill. He kept right on drinking.

"But I'm thirsty," said Liza. Bill paid her no attention. Suddenly Liza got mad. She pushed Bill. She pushed him hard. And into the stream he went. Then Bill got mad.

"That does it, Liza," he said. He came out of the stream, picked up Liza and dropped her in the water. He said, "You think you can push everybody around."

Liza caught his leg and pulled him back in. He landed on top of her. The two began to fight.

"Go right ahead," said Jed. "Just kill each other. I'm going to get a drink. Then I'm going to figure out this puzzle. You can stay there all day."

Liza and Bill glared at each other. Then Liza began to laugh. She said, "Boy, are you a mess."

"You should see yourself," said Bill. He began to laugh, too.

"Here," said Liza, "Put your head down. Let me wash out the sand."

"You won't duck me?" asked Bill.

"Promise," said Liza. The two began to clean each other up. After that, they climbed out of the stream.

"Gosh," said Bill. "That made me thirsty all over again."

36

He started for the spring. Then he stopped and said, "I'm just teasing. You get your drink."

Liza did. She said, "Okay, you can have the spring. I'm going to help Jed. And, I hope, get dry."

"Have you found anything, Jed?" called Bill.

"Nope," said Jed. "Sure could use some help."

"At your service," said Liza. "But what do we do?"

"Just what it says," said Jed. "Try to find blue."

Suddenly Bill called, "Hey, look up!"

Liza and Jed looked. Liza said, "What are we supposed to see?"

"Blue," said Bill. "Nobody can say that sky isn't blue."

"Ah, come on, Bill," said Liza.

"Yeah," said Jed. "I don't think that's exactly what Grandpa meant."

Bill laughed and said, "At least it's blue."

But Jed and Liza were too busy searching to even answer him. Then Jelly Bean starting yapping and going around in circles by a tree.

"Now what?" said Liza. She went over to see what he'd found. Then she laughed. Jelly Bean was bouncing around on the ground. And a squirrel was sitting on a limb above, scolding him.

"All right," said Liza. "Have your fun. At least the squirrel won't get you into any trouble."

She looked down at Jelly Bean. Then she saw something else.

"Jed, Bill!" she called. The boys ran to her. Liza was kneeling by a patch of blue violets.

"I think I found it," she said. The three looked through the patch carefully.

"Whoops!" said Bill, pushing the other two aside. He pulled out a small blue card.

"Hooray!" he shouted.

"Hooray for Jelly Bean, you mean," said Jed.

"Hooray for everybody," said Bill.

"What does it say?" asked Liza. She was hopping around as much as Jelly Bean.

"Green!" said Bill. "Grandpa seems to be determined to teach us our colors."

"Where's the map, Liza?" asked Jed.

Liza looked blank as she said, "I don't know."

"I hope you didn't drop it in the stream," said Jed.

Liza started running. The boys followed.

"I'll look around the spring," said Jed. "You follow the stream. If we can't find it, we'll have to go back to the cave and do another one."

Liza and Bill didn't argue. They started looking.

"There it is," said Liza. "It's caught in those weeds."

"Now that's what I call luck," said Bill. He got a stick and fished the map out of the stream.

"Is it okay?" asked Liza.

"Yep," said Bill. "Just a little wet."

"That makes three of us," said Liza. "Hey, Jed! We found it!"

Jed ran to where they were.

"Where do we go next?" he asked.

"The sweetheart tree," said Bill.

The "sweetheart tree" was an old hickory. The family called it the initial tree because long ago everyone had carved their initials on it. But to the children it was the sweetheart tree for a special reason. One summer when Gran was a little girl, she had been invited to spend the summer on the island. Grandpa's sister was her best friend. His older brother loved to tease her. So one day he carved a heart on the tree and put Gran and Grandpa's initials in it. Then he told Gran he had a surprise to show her. When Gran saw the heart, she was so embarrassed she wouldn't even go down for supper that night. She didn't dream that someday she and Grandpa would get married.

The children had to do some thinking to get their line of direction. They had never been to the sweetheart tree from the cave before. But it didn't take them long to get their bearings.

"It has to be over this way," said Jed, and started walking. Sure enough, they found it in just a few minutes.

"I didn't realize it was that close to the cave," said Liza.

"You know what?" said Bill.

"We've been through this before," said Liza. "Yes, I know 'what.' "

"Caught me on that one, didn't you?" said Bill. "To put

it in other words, I think we should carve our initials on the tree."

"Good idea," said Jed. "But not now. We have to find 'green.' "

"That's a tough one," said Liza. "Almost everything is green."

"It sure is," said Bill. "Do we have to look at every leaf? That's as bad as punching all of those bricks when we were trying to figure out if our house was haunted."

"I don't think Grandpa would make it that hard," said Jed.

"I have a feeling it has to do with the sweetheart tree," said Bill.

"I was thinking the same thing," said Liza.

"Then let's concentrate on it," said Jed. "He knows we don't have a ladder, so I'll bet it's within our reach."

The tree was old and big. There were plenty of hiding places. On hands and knees, the children searched.

"Hey, luck's with us," said Jed. Quickly Liza and Bill went to where he was. Jed said, "See that little corner of light green?"

"Where?" asked Bill. Jed pointed to a piece of green ground moss. A small corner of lighter green stuck out of it.

"Wow! What sharp eyes you have, Grandpa," said Bill. "I looked here and I didn't see that."

"That's nothing new," said Liza.

"Everybody can't be as smart as you," said Bill. He patted her on the head. Liza hated that. She started to say something, but Jed said, "Cut it out, you two. Don't you want to know what the card says?"

"I'm all ears," said Bill. "What color do we learn next?"

"Listen to this," said Jed, laughing. "Purple!"

"Purple!" said Liza and Bill. All three children laughed.

Bill said, "But that's Grandpa's most unfavorite color."

"And where do we look for this 'purple?' " asked Jed. Liza looked at the map.

"The inlet!" she said.

"You've got to be kidding," said Bill. "What is Grandpa trying to do to us?"

"Obviously, wear us out," said Jed. "Let's go."

This time the children did not run. Jelly Bean just stood still and yapped.

"Now what?" said Liza. Jelly Bean looked at them.

"I think he's tired," said Jed. He picked up the puppy. Jelly Bean snuggled in his arms and was quiet.

"I wish that would work for me," said Bill. "I'd stand there yapping, too."

"Sorry, old boy," said Liza. "But you'll just have to yap by yourself."

"That seems to be the story of my life," said Bill. "Let's go."

41

It took them a while to reach the inlet. They called it their private swimming pool. When they got there, all three just flopped on the sand.

"Purple will just have to wait," said Liza.

"Right now I don't care if we never find purple," said Bill.

"I wonder why Grandpa chose that color," said Jed. "He says he hates it."

"Remember when Gran bought a purple dress?" asked Liza.

"I sure do," said Jed, laughing. "And I remember how quickly it was returned to the store."

Suddenly Bill sat up. He said, "I think I know why he chose it. So many of the sea shells have some purple on them."

"Ugh!" said Jed. "Do we have to look under every shell?"

"Now would Grandpa do that to us?" asked Bill.

"I don't know," said Jed. "Can you think of anything else it could be?"

The children lay back on the sand. Suddenly Jed yelled, "Whoopee!"

He jumped up.

"What?" said Liza and Bill.

"That big beach towel," said Jed. "Remember, it has stripes on it and the biggest one is purple."

"Yeah," said Bill. "Grandpa didn't like it. But it was the only one Gran could find that was large enough."

"And he always leaves it under those scrub bushes," said Liza.

The children ran to the bush. Sure enough, there was the towel. Pinned to the purple stripe was a small card.

"What does it say?" asked Bill. "I can't see."

"Blue and white," said Jed. "That's a new one."

"Okay," said Bill. "Where is blue and white?"

Liza was already looking at the map. She said, "The scraggly red bush."

"Hooray!" said Bill. "At least that gets us home."

Even Jelly Bean seemed ready to go. It didn't take long to get from the inlet to the house. The children didn't go in. They ran straight to the scraggly bush with red flowers. They knew that bush well. It had been a clue in the treasure hunt.

"And we don't even have to look for blue and white," shouted Bill. Hanging on the bush was a sheet of white paper with blue writing on it.

"Quick, Bill," said Liza. "Read it."

Bill read, "Get yourselves cleaned up and come to Mrs. Hawkins's house at five o'clock. Love, Gran and Grandpa."

"What does that mean?" asked Liza.

"I don't know," said Jed. "But we'd better hurry. It's four-thirty now."

"We sure do need to clean up," said Liza. The children went into the house. Each was wondering what the next surprise would be.

7

Surprise

"I've got to take a shower," said Liza. "I'm really a mess."

"Well, be quick about it," said Bill. "I was in that stream, too."

The children wasted no time getting cleaned up and into fresh clothes.

"This really is a wild day," said Jed. "What do you suppose is going to happen next?"

"Now that we've learned our colors," said Bill, "maybe Grandpa is going to teach us our numbers."

"Do you suppose all grandparents are as much fun as ours?" asked Liza.

"No," said Jed. "At least none of the grandparents of kids I know are."

"But maybe they don't have as charming grandchildren as ours do," said Bill.

"Well, charming or not," said Jed, "we had better hurry. It's almost five o'clock."

The children ran the short distance to Widow Hawkins's house. Jed looked at his watch and said, "Five o'clock on the dot."

Liza knocked. Immediately Widow Hawkins opened the door.

"Here you are," she said. "Your grandfather was afraid you wouldn't make it. Come on in."

The children went in. Then they stopped and stared in surprise. The room was all decorated and filled with people. Suddenly the people began to sing, "Happy early birthday to you."

The children were too stunned to say anything. Grandpa laughed and said, "I would say this is one surprise party that really is a surprise."

"You can bet on that!" said Bill.

"Oh, it's all so pretty!" said Liza.

"We don't get much entertainment here," said Widow Hawkins. "So we jump at the chance to have a party."

"You really made sure we would be out of the way, Grandpa," said Bill.

"Don't say a word," said Gran. "He's been worried all afternoon for fear he made your puzzle too difficult."

"Now, Gran," said Grandpa. "I wasn't that worried. These three always manage somehow. Besides, I left a note on the kitchen table just in case."

Liza was looking around at all the people. Widow

Hawkins noticed. She said, "Oh, dear, where are my manners? I haven't even introduced the children. These are some of the regular islanders. Of course, you all know these are Liza, Jed and Bill."

"Ah, come on, Jenny," said one man. "Let us introduce ourselves. They will never remember all the names at once."

"All right," said Widow Hawkins. "We'll start with you."

"That's better. I'm Captain Ned," said the man. "I roved the seas all my young days. Then I took myself a wife and settled here."

"I'm the wife he took. Everybody just calls me Nora," said the woman next to him.

"Gee, Captain Ned," said Bill, "were you a pirate?"

"We'll get together one of these first days, young man," said Captain Ned. "I've got some good stories to tell."

"Just don't believe everything," said Nora. "His stories change with each telling."

"So do Bill's," said Liza. Everybody laughed. Then the other people introduced themselves. But after Captain Ned they sounded dull. Liza kept looking around.

"Where's Hermit Dan?" she asked. "Wasn't he invited?"

"He certainly was," said Grandpa. "I invited him myself."

"Dan doesn't take much to being with people," said Captain Ned.

"But he did something very unusual for him," said Widow Hawkins. She went into the kitchen. She came back with a basket.

"Raspberries!" said Liza.

"Yes," said Widow Hawkins. "He said they were for you."

The children looked at each other. All three felt guilty.

"Okay," said Grandpa, "something's up. Out with it."

"We went in his garden this morning," said Jed.

"And we started to pick some raspberries," said Liza.

"But only Liza got one before he chased us out," said Bill.

"You mean you went in his garden without asking?" said Gran.

"But it's your land," said Bill.

"It's his garden," said Grandpa, "and he has permission to use the land."

"I bet he gave it to you good," said Captain Ned, laughing. "I've seen him tell some of the summer kids off."

"He sure did," said Bill with a big grin.

"Twice," said Jed.

"Twice!" said Grandpa. "What else did you get into?"

"Jelly Bean found a nest of baby rabbits," said Liza. "We wanted to take them home for pets."

"He really let us have it then," said Bill. "And he said you should teach us about island life."

"He's right about that," said Grandpa. "I should give you some ground rules."

"He shouted at us," said Liza. "But it wasn't mean shouting. He explained why we shouldn't take the rabbits."

"That's Dan, all right," said Nora. "He has great respect for nature's ways. He makes sure we all go by them."

"Dan might sound gruff," said someone else, "but he's the kindest person I've ever known."

"Did he get after you with his stick?" asked Captain Ned.

"He started waving it around," said Jed. "But I don't think he would have hit us."

"Then he must like you," said Captain Ned.

"He sure has a funny way of showing it," said Bill.

"That's enough about Dan," said Widow Hawkins. "Do come in the dining room and serve yourselves."

Everybody moved then. In the dining room, Bill's eyes got bigger and bigger. He said, "I never saw so much food."

"The early birthdayers go first," said Widow Hawkins.

She did not have to say more. Bill grabbed a plate and

took some of everything. Grandpa laughed and said, "You'll never make it through all of that."

"Want to bet?" said Bill.

"I'll bet you'll have a stomachache if you do," said Gran.

"Nope," said Bill. "That's not my kind of bet."

8

Questions for Grandpa

Bill was true to his word. He cleaned up his plate. After the dishes were stacked, Widow Hawkins said, "All right. Is everybody ready?"

The others nodded. She went into the kitchen. She came back with a huge birthday cake covered with candles.

"Oh, look!" said Liza.

"Oh, no!" groaned Bill.

"We didn't know how many candles to put on for the three of you," said Widow Hawkins, "so we just put as many as we could."

"Okay, kids," said Captain Ned, "show your wind and make a wish."

The children blew, and every candle flickered out. All the guests clapped.

"Gee," said Jed, "we never had a real birthday party like this."

"And there's home-churned ice cream, too," said Gran.

"Why didn't somebody tell me this was coming?" said Bill. "Please, just a little bit for me."

Gran looked at Bill. She said, "You can take the cake home and eat it later."

"It wouldn't be the same, Gran," said Bill. "Birthday cake should be eaten at the party."

Soon after the cake and ice cream, the party broke up. Widow Hawkins would accept no help with the cleaning up. "But Liza," she said, "don't forget the raspberries."

"Thanks for reminding me," said Liza. She got the basket.

Bill groaned all the way home. He said, "I'm glad I didn't take you up on that stomachache bet, Gran. You sure would have won."

"I know," said Gran. "I'll fix you up as soon as we get home."

They walked the rest of the way in silence. Everybody was tired and caught up in their own thoughts.

It wasn't a long walk and soon they were in the house. Jelly Bean started prancing and yapping when he heard them.

"Here you are, Jelly Bean," said Liza. "I brought you a piece of cake."

Jelly Bean quickly gobbled it up. He looked at Liza for more.

"No," said Liza. "That's all."

Bill was on the sofa, groaning.

"I'm surprised Bill just has a stomachache," said Jed. "With all he ate, he should have exploded."

"I feel like I am going to," said Bill.

Gran went to the kitchen. She took out the baking soda and mixed a very strong dose of it. Then she went to Bill.

"All right, dear," she said. "You won't like this, but it will make you feel better."

"What is it?" asked Bill.

"Very strong soda water," said Gran.

"Give it to me," said Bill. "I'll take anything right now."

"Not here," said Gran. "In the bathroom."

"Why?" asked Bill.

"Because it will make you throw up," said Gran.

"But that's worse than the stomachache," said Bill.

"No," said Gran. "It will relieve the pressure in your stomach. Then you'll feel better. Come on now. No nonsense."

Bill followed Gran to the bathroom.

"All right," said Gran. "Drink it all."

Bill did, and said, "Ugh, that's awful."

But he had time to say no more. He ran to the toilet bowl and began to throw up. Gran got a wet wash cloth and put it to his head. Bill threw up again and again. Then suddenly he looked up at Gran and smiled.

"No more stomachache," he said. "But all that good food wasted."

"Oh, I don't know," said Gran. "You had the fun of eating it."

"Right you are, Gran," said Bill. "And stomachache or not, I would do it again."

"I'm sure you would," said Gran. "Now go lie down on the sofa and rest."

They went back into the living room. Liza and Jed were on the sofa.

"Off," said Bill.

"Why?" asked Liza. "It's not your sofa."

"Gran told me to lie down on it and rest," said Bill.

Liza looked at Gran.

"He's right," said Gran. "He needs to give his stomach time to settle down."

"Oh," said Liza. She and Jed slid to the floor.

"Grandpa," said Liza, "please tell us all you know about Hermit Dan."

Grandpa thought a minute.

"Well, let me see," he said. "I don't know too much about him. His family was quite well-to-do, but they sort of stayed to themselves. They had a beautiful home. I don't remember just when it burned down, but it was after his parents died."

"Did you like him?" asked Bill.

"Yes," said Grandpa. "He was a little older than me. He was just as nice a boy as you would want."

54

"But what made him change?" asked Jed.

"That part is a mystery to me," said Grandpa. "He had two older sisters. I know all three children left the island at some time, but nobody seems to know where they went. Dan came back a number of years ago. He built himself that little shack and has very little to do with people. He did write and ask if he could use our land for a garden. I told him he was welcome to it. We fish at the same spot. Sometimes he speaks to me. Other times he just nods. The only time he's asked me for anything was to help in fencing over his garden. But he didn't say a half dozen words while we worked. I talked to him. But it was a one-way conversation."

"One thing for sure," said Liza. "He can't hate children as much as he pretends. If he did, he wouldn't have given us those raspberries."

"Just don't do anything like that again," said Gran.

"We found out about rabbits today," said Bill. "Is there anything else about the island we should know?"

"As a matter of fact, there is," said Grandpa. "I've been meaning to talk to you."

"And I've been meaning to remind you," said Gran.

"For goodness sake!" said Bill. "Then one of you talk to us."

"A little patience, lad," said Grandpa. "At least we know you feel well again when you get that impatient tone."

"It's about sandstorms," said Gran.

"Oh," said Grandpa, "I take it you're going to tell them."

"No," said Gran. "Just trying to get you started."

The children laughed.

"All right, all right," said Grandpa. "So I'm too slow. Every so often the island is hit by a sandstorm. It starts out like a big whirlwind and with no warning. It can be very dangerous. If you get caught in one, run to the nearest house you see. It doesn't matter whether you know who lives there or not. They will take you in. Stay there until they tell you it's all right to go out."

"But," said Jed, "suppose we're in the woods?"

56

"That's not quite as bad," said Grandpa. "The winds get high, but there's not much sand. Try to get to the cave if you're too far away to get to the house."

"Do these happen often?" asked Liza.

"No," said Grandpa. "But they are more likely to happen in summer than winter."

"I think we can handle that," said Jed. "Anything else?"

"I don't think so," said Grandpa. "Anything to add, Gran?"

"No," said Gran, "not at the moment."

"Grandpa," said Bill, "is it all right if we go down to the other end of the island? I'd like to see what it's like."

"I think that's a fine idea," said Gran. "There are several children there. You may make some new friends."

"But I still want to know more about Hermit Dan," said Liza. "Do you suppose Widow Hawkins could tell us anything?"

"Possibly," said Grandpa. "It wouldn't hurt to ask her."

"I know," said Bill, popping up. "Captain Ned. I'll bet he knows something."

"If there's anything to know, he will," said Grandpa. "Ned likes to know everything."

"And he also likes to talk," said Gran.

Liza looked out of the window. She said, "I wish it wasn't night. I want to go now."

"Well, Miss Impatience," said Gran, "there's just one place you're going now. And that's to bed."

"Ahh, Gran," said Bill.

"No ahh, Gran, from you, young man," said Gran. "You've had a big day. Whatever Captain Ned knows will keep until tomorrow."

"You're a hard one to get around," said Bill. He stretched and yawned.

"Proof," said Jed. "Gran's right. I'm going to bed."

It wasn't long before the Roberts house was quiet. Only the night sounds broke the silence.

9
Captain Ned's Story

The children were up bright and early the next morning. After breakfast, Jed said, "Who wants a swim?"

"I do," said Liza. "We missed out completely yesterday."

"But what about Captain Ned?" asked Bill. Liza and Jed looked at each other. They had forgotten that.

"You've got all day," said Gran. "Have a swim and then visit."

"Okay, Bill?" asked Liza.

"Let's get into our swimsuits," said Bill.

Soon the three were running to the inlet. Bill didn't stop when he got to the water. He dived right in and started swimming.

Later, Liza said, "I've had enough. I'm going to get dressed."

"Oh, no, you don't, Liza," said Bill. "We all go

together. You're not going to Captain Ned's without us."

Liza blushed. That was exactly what she had planned to do.

"Then come on," she said. "I want to hear what he has to say."

It didn't take the children long to get themselves ready to go to Captain Ned's.

Liza knocked at the door. Nora answered. She said, "Well, it's the birthday children. Come in, come in."

"Is Captain Ned here?" asked Bill.

"Of course I'm here," said Captain Ned. "Where did you expect me to be?"

Then he roared with laughter. The children didn't know quite what to say. But Captain Ned took care of that. He asked, "Can I do something for you?"

"Yes, sir," said Jed. "At least we hope so. Would you mind telling us what you know about Hermit Dan?"

"Oh, it's Dan you're curious about," said Captain Ned. "He's a real puzzler all right. I've known him all my life. But I don't know the man he is now."

"When did he change?" asked Bill.

"I don't know exactly," said Captain Ned. "After I finished school, I went to sea. For a number of years, I had no contact with him. He loved the island and the family home. He said he would never leave it. The house was beautiful. Dan planned to turn it into a museum someday."

"Were you here when it burned down?" asked Jed.

60

"No," said Captain Ned. "About the only person I kept in touch with was Jenny Hawkins. Being at sea, it was sometimes months before I would get her letters. Her husband died suddenly of a heart attack. Within days, Dan's mother also died. Dan had two older sisters, but they had left the island when they finished school. They never returned after their parents died. Dan stayed on. But when the house burned, he left. He was gone for years and kept in contact with no one. When Nora and I got married, we decided to settle down and came back to the island. I was an only child, so I inherited the family property. About a year later, Dan came back."

"How was he then?" asked Bill.

"Just the way he is now," said Captain Ned.

"Do you think he had a wife and children?" asked Liza.

"I have a feeling he had a wife," said Captain Ned. "Sometimes I can get Dan to talk a bit. Usually it's just about the weather or his garden. But one day he slipped up and said, 'wife.' Then he walked away quickly. Do you know of anything I left out, Nora?"

"No," said Nora. "I wish we could help him. He's so good to other people."

"Oh," said Captain Ned, "there is one more thing. Once a month Dan goes to Mainland. That's the only time he ever leaves the island."

"He gets to be more and more of a mystery," said Jed.

"Is it true that his ancestors were pirates?" asked Bill.

"That's what Dan used to say when he was a boy," said Captain Ned. "He said that's why his family had money. He said they were the first ones to settle on the island and were the ones who named it Pirate Island. He was quite proud of it."

"I didn't know that," said Nora.

"Do you think it's true?" asked Bill. His eyes were shining

"I don't know," said Captain Ned. "His folks were nice people, but they didn't mingle much with the other islanders. When I was about your age, I asked his mother if the stories Dan told were true. She just looked at me and said she was sure the island held many secrets. I wanted to question her more, but her look stopped me."

"Thanks a lot," said Jed. "We didn't know any of that."

"Can't you stay awhile?" asked Nora. "We do like children. We have grandchildren around your age. They should be coming to visit soon."

"Boys or girls?" asked Liza.

"Both," said Captain Ned.

"Good," said Liza. "I get tired of being the only girl."

"We have to go now," said Jed.

"But we'll come back," said Liza.

"Yes," said Bill. "I want to hear some of your stories, Captain Ned."

"Anytime," said Captain Ned.

The children said their good-byes and left.

'Why the rush to get away?" asked Bill. "I like them."

"So do I," said Jed. "But I thought this would be a good chance to look around that shack Hermit Dan lives in. He's sure to be at his garden at this time of day."

"You remember what Grandpa said," said Liza.

"Oh, come on, Liza," said Bill. "You know what Jed means. We won't go in or anything. We could just peek in the windows. That wouldn't hurt, would it? Grandpa just said to stay out of his garden."

Curiosity got the best of Liza. She grinned and said, "Let's go!"

"Hey, look at those neat dunes," said Bill. "I never noticed them before."

"We've never been in this direction before," said Jed. Bill ran ahead and scrambled to the top of one. He shouted, "King of the mountain!"

Liza and Jed followed him. The children began a lively game. Each tried to push the others from the top and become king. But their game was abruptly stopped.

"Get off my dunes!" shouted Hermit Dan. "Get off right now."

The children scrambled down. Hermit Dan was angry, really angry. He waved his stick in all directions.

"So it's you brats again," he said. "Can't get my work done for having to guard my property against brats. Get off my dunes and stay off. Did you get that? Stay away!"

"All right, all right!" shouted Bill angrily. Liza and Jed were too stunned to say anything. Bill stalked away. They just followed.

"I never met anyone that mean before," said Bill. "What's so special about those dunes?"

"Maybe they are a part of the mystery of Hermit Dan," said Jed.

"I was thinking the same thing," said Liza.

With that, Bill forgot about being angry. He asked, "Do you really think so? Maybe we better stake out this place."

"How can we?" asked Liza. "You remember what Gran and Grandpa said."

"Sure," said Bill. "They said to stay out of his way. I intend to do that. That stick came mighty close to me once or twice. But this makes it more important to investigate the dunes and that shack."

64

Jed, too, began to get excited. He said, "Let's go down to the summer people's end of the island. Later we'll sit down and write out the facts we know."

"Good idea," said Liza. "Then we can make a plan."

"But why not now?" asked Bill. "Why wait?"

"Because it will give us time to think," said Liza.

"Not only that," said Jed. "Remember this is our first visit to the island. Some of the summer kids have had run-ins with him. They may be able to tell us something."

"Yeah," said Bill. "I never thought about that."

10

The Summer Children

Liza, Jed and Bill heard laughing and squealing as they neared the summer people's end of the island. They soon saw why. A group of children were playing dodge ball.

"That looks like fun," said Bill. "Think they'll let us play?"

"Let's wait until they finish this game and ask," said Liza.

"We may be able to get up a softball team," said Jed. "There should be enough for a good game."

"Great," said Bill. "This is going to be a good summer."

Just then two big boys came along. One pushed a little girl out of the way and took the ball.

"Hey, Hank," he shouted, "catch."

He threw the ball to the other boy.

"Nice throw, Ted," said Hank.

The children who had been playing watched as the two boys ran off with the ball.

"What's the matter with those kids?" said Bill. "Why are they letting them take their ball?"

"I don't know," said Jed. "It may belong to the boys. Let's ask."

The dodge-ball players just plopped on the sand. Liza, Bill and Jed walked over to them. They heard one say, "There ought to be some way to stop them."

"But how?" said another.

"Hi," said Jed. "Okay if we join you?"

The children looked up and smiled.

"Sure, sit down," said a red-haired boy. "I'm Peter James."

"I'm Jed Roberts. This is my sister, Liza, and my brother, Bill," said Jed. The other children all introduced themselves.

"Which house is yours?" asked Suzy. "I didn't know any were vacant."

"We're visiting our grandparents," said Liza. "Their house is at the other end of the island."

The children's eyes opened wide.

"You mean up where that crazy man lives?" asked Jack.

"If you mean Hermit Dan, yes," said Jed.

"That's the one," said Steve.

"But we live farther up," said Jed. "Our house is the last one at that end of the island."

"Aren't you afraid of him?" asked Peter.

"Sort of," said Liza. "We just try to stay out of his way."

"Has he ever gotten after you with that stick?" asked Marie.

Liza, Bill and Jed laughed. Bill said, "Has he ever!"

"And not too many minutes ago," said Liza. "We were playing on his dunes."

"The dunes!" said Suzy. "Remember what happened to us, Jason?"

"I sure do," said Jason. "When we came here for our first summer, nobody told us about him. We love to explore. A few of us decided to go to the other end of the island. We saw the dunes and stopped to play on them. Suddenly this madman came running out waving a stick. He told us never to come near his dunes or that end of the island, just to go back where we belonged."

"Scared us half to death," said Suzy. "We sure didn't argue. We told our parents about it. They talked to some other people. It seems there's sort of an invisible line we aren't supposed to cross."

"And we don't cross that line, either," said Suzy. "Is he a pirate like some say?"

"Nobody seems to know much about him," said Rebecca.

68

"We don't know much either," said Jed. "He's not a pirate. But there is a story that some of his ancestors were."

"Okay, children, here's your little ball," said Hank. The children hadn't heard the older boys come back. Then Ted put the ball on the ground and stomped on it as hard as he could. The ball exploded like a balloon. The boys walked away.

At first the children couldn't say anything. Then Marie said, "They popped my ball. And I just got it, too." She was almost in tears.

"We saw them take the ball," said Jed. "You didn't even try to stop them. Why?"

"You can't stop them," said Peter. "They're as mean as they come. This is their first time here."

"And I hope it's their last," said Janet. "They make life miserable for us."

"But why couldn't you stop them?" asked Bill. "There are more of you."

"I know," said John. "But they fight to hurt. We just end up with bloody noses."

"How can they beat you all at once?" asked Bill. "Come on, Jed, let's go get them."

"No, don't!" said the children.

"You see," said Amy, "they wait until they see one or two of us alone and then they beat us up."

"Can't you talk to your parents?" asked Liza.

"We did," said Steve, "and they talked to the boys' parents. But the parents are just as bad. They just said children are bound to have their fights."

"So our parents said to just let them be and not fight back," said Jane.

"Usually they just break up our games. Then they get bored and leave. This is the first time they've ever done anything like this," said Suzy.

"I think they're mad because we saw what happened yesterday," said Peter.

"What happened?" asked Jed.

"They had heard about Hermit Dan," said Jason. "And they started boasting. They said no crazy man was going to stop them. They would go anywhere they wanted to. They would tear down those dunes if they liked."

"And then what?" asked Bill.

"They said they would go then," said Amy. "We could go along and watch if we weren't too scared."

"So we decided to follow them," said Ed. "Or at least four of us did. We stayed way behind them."

"Oh, do hurry," said Liza. "What happened?"

"They marched right up to the dunes," said Peter. "We hid behind some bushes. But we could see everything."

"Then Hank and Ted just went crazy," said Suzy. "They started yelling, 'Crazy old man, crazy old man. Come on out, catch us if you can.'"

"And all the time they were pulling up the grass on the dunes and kicking the sand," said Janet.

70

"Nothing happened at first," said Peter, "and we thought the old man wasn't there. Then he came and, boy, can he move. But Hank and Ted kept right on."

"The old man ran right up those dunes and started hitting them," said Ed. "And he hit hard. He was so fast that Hank and Ted just covered their eyes with their hands. They couldn't seem to move. Then the old man slowed down and they started running. But they yelled back at him. They said he had better watch out. They were going to get even with him. They ran right past where we were hiding."

"I'm glad Hermit Dan beat them," said Liza. "They deserved it."

"He hurt them enough to make them cry," said Suzy, "and they knew we saw them. So now they're taking it out on us."

"That's awful," said Bill. "Hermit Dan isn't really mean. They had no right to do that to him. They made him hit them."

"Why do you say he's not really mean?" asked Amy. "You said he chased you with that stick."

"Yes," said Jed. "But it was our fault. We knew we weren't supposed to go around his place."

Then Liza told them how he was with the islanders and about the raspberries. The children were surprised to hear all of this.

"Gee," said Marie, "he sounds like a nice person. But why does he act so mean to children?"

"Maybe it's because he's old and we are noisy," said Ed. "He's not used to having children around."

"Noisy we are," said Bill. "Hermit Dan loves the island, but—"

"Hey, look at the time," interrupted Jed. "Gran and Grandpa will be wondering where we are."

Liza and Bill looked surprised. Jed didn't usually interrupt unless there was some good reason. So they took their cue from him.

Bill said, "I thought my stomach was trying to tell me something."

"We really had better go," said Liza. "But I'm sure glad we met you all."

"Will you come back soon?" asked Peter.

"We sure will," said Bill. "Do you like to play soft-ball?"

"Yes!" shouted Amy. "Trouble is, we don't have a bat or a ball."

"We do," said Jed. "We'll bring them down."

"When?" asked Paul. "I do love softball."

"We'll try to come tomorrow," said Jed. "But we really do have to go now."

The children started away.

"Why the sudden rush?" asked Bill. "Is it really that late?"

"It is late," said Jed. "But I didn't want you to say anything else."

"Why not?" asked Bill.

"Because then they might want to join in solving this mystery," said Jed. "And Hank and Ted would be sure to find out. We'd better do this alone."

"That makes sense," said Bill. "I must be improving. I figured out you must have a reason. Did you notice I didn't even argue?"

73

"I did," said Jed. "You surprised me."

"But I'm worried about Hermit Dan," said Liza. "Suppose Hank and Ted do try to get even? I don't want anything to happen to him."

"And they're mean enough to hurt him," said Bill. "Look what they did to Marie's new ball."

"I was thinking about that, too," said Jed. "I think we should tell Grandpa about that. Maybe he will know what to do. Hank and Ted could spy on Hermit Dan and find out when he's not there and wreck his place."

"Let's move fast," said Liza.

"First, let's move fast toward lunch," said Bill. "I'm starving."

He started running. Liza and Jed joined him. But then they had to slow down. It was a longer way than they had thought.

11

A Concerned Grandpa

The children talked as they walked.

"There has to be something about those dunes," said Bill. "I think we should make sure he's not there, and do some investigating."

"We've got a lot of planning to do," said Jed. "I think you're right about those dunes. But we also have to try to protect Hermit Dan."

"Maybe we should take turns watching his place when he's not there," said Liza.

"That's an idea," said Bill, "but we have to be careful and keep out of sight."

"Anyway," said Jed, "I'm glad we talked with those kids. I have a feeling that Hank and Ted don't forget things that make them mad."

"Maybe we should talk to Widow Hawkins," said Liza.

"I think she's about Hermit Dan's best friend. Remember the deal they have?"

"What deal?" asked Bill and Jed together.

"You know," said Liza. "That first time we had lunch there. She said Hermit Dan brought her food and she canned it."

"So what?" said Bill. "He seems to take food to all the islanders."

"Yes," said Liza. "But when she cans it, they divide it. That's the deal."

"Now I remember," said Jed. "I'll bet she does other things for him, too. You're right, Liza. We'll visit her after lunch."

The children finally got home.

"My," said Gran, "you must have been having fun. Grandpa and I have already had lunch. But yours is on the table."

"Thanks, Gran," said Liza as she hugged her.

"I'm sure ready for it," said Bill.

"We went down to the other end of the island," said Liza.

"There are a lot of nice kids there," said Jed.

"I had a feeling that's where you were," said Grandpa. "I'm glad you found some new friends. Gran and I want to get down there and meet some of the people."

"One family is awful," said Bill.

"What happened?" asked Gran.

The children told them about Hank and Ted. Grandpa looked concerned. He said, "I don't like the sound of that."

"Neither did we," said Liza.

"Did you happen to get their last names?" asked Grandpa.

"No," said Jed. "But they're brothers."

"I had better talk to Captain Ned about that," said Grandpa. "We don't need that kind of people on the island. Most of the people own their houses. Ned checks out the other people very carefully before he rents to them."

"But what can he do?" asked Jed. "He can't make them leave, can he?"

"I don't know," said Grandpa. "But if they're in one of the rented houses, he may be able to do something. Ned owns all that end of the island. At least he can warn the boys and their parents. I've never heard of anything like this happening before."

"Ned is a good businessman," said Gran. "Didn't he put some kind of protective clause in the contract when he sold those houses?"

"That's right, he did," said Grandpa. "I forget the wording, but it means if the buyers prove to be undesirable Ned can buy the house back for the same price at which he sold it. So you see, he can do something."

"I hope he does it quickly," said Jed. "We're worried about Hermit Dan."

"I'm surprised Hermit Dan even speaks to Captain Ned for letting all those people come," said Bill.

"Dan didn't like it," said Grandpa. "But Ned's son is a contractor. He talked Ned into it. That's why there is a wide strip of land between those houses and the islanders. But Ned realized it would help the islanders. They were to be given the jobs of caretakers when the summer people weren't here. That was a part of the deal. Some of them

78

were having a hard time making ends meet. This gave them a chance to pick up a few extra dollars."

"Gee," said Liza. "The islanders do so much for each other."

"Indeed they do," said Gran. "That's what makes this place so special."

"That's why this concerns me so much," said Grandpa. "We've never had any trouble." Then he chuckled and said, "Dan and his stick have the summer people well trained to stay away from this end of the island. But I'll speak to Ned this afternoon."

Bill had been quiet during this time. He was hungry and much too busy eating to join in.

"Ahh," he said, "that feels better. My stomach was so empty it was touching my backbone."

"I should never let you leave the house without a bag of food around your neck," said Gran.

"That's a good idea," said Bill. "Can we start today?"

"Eat, eat, eat," said Liza. "That's all you think about."

"But I'm supposed to be a growing boy," said Bill. "How can I grow without food?"

"The way you three stay on the go," said Gran, "I don't see how you grow at all. You burn up all the food running around."

"About running around," said Bill. "Didn't we say something about going swimming after lunch?"

"I don't remember," said Liza, "but I'm ready."

"Just hold it," said Gran. "Thirty minutes' rest first. At least give your lunch time to settle."

"Ahh, Gran," said Bill.

"By the time you do the dishes and get the kitchen in order the time will be up," said Gran. "Then you can have your swim and I'll go with Grandpa to Ned's. I feel like a visit with Nora."

"Oh, that reminds me," said Jed. "Do you think Widow Hawkins would mind if we visited her?"

"I'm sure she would love it," said Gran. "She said the other day she wished you would come more often. She enjoys children, and has none of her own."

"Good," said Bill. "We'll go after we swim."

Liza looked at Gran and grinned. Then she said, "Don't worry, we'll dress first."

"Now, how did you know what I was thinking?" asked Gran.

"The family says we're just alike," said Liza. "I guess that means in thinking, too."

Suddenly Bill started laughing. The others looked at him.

"I was just imagining the look on Widow Hawkins's face if we walked in dripping water everywhere," said Bill. "She might decide she doesn't enjoy children after all."

12

Widow Hawkins

Somehow the children couldn't get too interested in swimming. Questions kept piling up in their minds. It wasn't long before Jed said, "I'm not in the mood for swimming. I think I'll get dressed and start that list."

"I'll go with you," said Liza.

"I don't really want to swim, either," said Bill. "Let's go."

The children were back at the house before Gran and Grandpa left.

"That was a mighty short swim," said Grandpa. "Is anything wrong?"

"No," said Jed. "We're just tired."

"And besides," said Bill, "we want to find—"

Liza pinched him.

"Ouch! That hurt," said Bill. "Why did you pinch me?"

"I thought I saw a bug," said Liza.

"Well, you could have brushed it off," said Bill. Then he saw Liza wink and he knew she thought he was about to say the wrong thing. "But thanks, anyway," he said. "I don't want to be Buggy Bill."

They started to their rooms. Jed said, "You were almost Blabbermouth Bill. I'm glad Liza was close enough to stop you."

"Are we going to have to keep all kinds of secrets again?" asked Bill. "You know I have a hard time doing that."

"So do I," said Liza. "But I thought I better stop you until we decide what to do."

"Right," said Jed. "If we're going to keep guard over Hermit Dan's place, it will have to be a secret. You know Gran and Grandpa would say no to that."

"Yeah," said Bill. "And that was my idea. Guess you'll have to keep on pinching, Liza."

They dressed and started for Widow Hawkins's house.

Widow Hawkins must have been looking out of the window. As they walked up her steps, she opened the door.

"Oh, I was hoping you were coming to see me," she said.

"And here we are," said Bill, giving her a hug.

"Would you like some cookies and lemonade?" she said. "I baked this morning."

"That sounds awfully good," said Jed. "But we had a big lunch."

"How about you, Bill?" said Widow Hawkins. "You always seem to be able to eat."

"Maybe a little later," said Bill.

"Mrs. Hawkins," said Liza, "we're really curious about Hermit Dan. We were wondering if you would tell us what you know."

"Oh, dear," said Widow Hawkins, "has he been after you again?"

"It was our fault," said Jed. "We were playing on his dunes."

"Those dunes!" said Widow Hawkins. "You would think they were made of pure gold the way he protects them."

"We figured you would know more than anyone," said Jed. "And we're worried about him."

"Worried?" said Widow Hawkins. "Why?"

The children told her the story of Hank and Ted.

"That is enough to worry all of us," said Widow Hawkins. "No wonder he wouldn't even speak to me yesterday. He was busy planting more reeds on those dunes. I called to him, but he didn't even look up."

"He had a right to be mad at us," said Bill. "I wish we had known about the dunes."

"We thought maybe if you told us what you know about him we could help," said Liza.

Widow Hawkins thought for a minute. Then she said, "All right. Perhaps you can come up with something new. We would all like to help Dan, but he won't give us a chance. I was born and grew up on the island just as he did. In fact, my husband grew up here, too. We all went over to Mainland to school. There used to be more islanders here, but the young people began to leave when they finished school. Dan was just one of the group and everybody liked him."

"We talked to Captain Ned this morning," said Bill. "He said Hermit Dan had planned to make a museum out of the family home someday. He had said he would never leave the island."

"That's true," said Widow Hawkins. "Dan talked about his plans from the time he was very young."

"What was the house like?" asked Liza.

"Oh, it was a grand place," said Widow Hawkins. "We were all a bit in awe of it. Dan's parents were nice, but we were never invited inside the house."

"Never?" said Bill.

"I think I was in the living room twice the whole time the house was there. It was beautiful, and even as a child I knew it was filled with treasures. But even birthday parties were held outside or on the porch."

"But didn't you think that was strange?" asked Bill.

"No," said Widow Hawkins. "We just felt they were afraid we might break something or that we were too noisy. Dan and his sisters were rather quiet children."

"Do you think his ancestors were pirates?" asked Bill.

Widow Hawkins smiled and said, "Dan could tell some mighty convincing stories about them which we liked to believe. They could very well have been pirates. But nobody has any proof of it."

"I believe they were," said Bill, "and I'm going to find proof of it."

Liza and Jed frowned at Bill. They knew he would go on and on. But he saw their look and stopped.

"This other problem is more important now," said Jed. "Were you here when the house burned?"

"Yes," said Widow Hawkins. A pained look came on her face. "But Dan wasn't. He had gone to Mainland for something." She shook her head. "It was terrible, and so sudden. The house seemed to explode into flames. We did what we could, but we had no fire-fighting equipment. Dan arrived in the middle of it. He was like a wild man. He ran right through the flames and came out holding a box. His hair was on fire. He looked burned all over."

"Poor man!" said Liza.

"Yes," said Widow Hawkins. "But it wasn't as bad as it could have been. We wanted to take him over to Mainland to the hospital. But he would not go. Old Aunt Gussie had been a nurse. She looked after his burns. She said they weren't as bad as they looked at first."

"What was in the box?" asked Bill.

"That we never found out," said Widow Hawkins. "Dan would let no one touch it. He kept screaming to catch those two boys he had passed coming home. Dan had his own boat then. He kept saying the two boys had done it."

"What two boys?" asked Liza.

"That we didn't know," said Widow Hawkins. "At first we just thought Dan was out of his head because of the burns. But he kept talking about those boys. Someone went over to Mainland and got the police. We had no telephone then."

"Did they believe Hermit Dan?" asked Jed.

"They didn't question him at first, but looked around the ruins of the house. They found some rag torches that had been soaked in oil. They found some other things, too, but I don't know what they were. The fire was definitely started on purpose."

"What did the police do then?" asked Bill.

"By that time Dan had quieted down and could talk to them. It seems four young people had come over one day and wanted to go through the house. Dan wouldn't let them. Two of the boys got very angry. Then a few days later, Dan caught those two trying to rob the house. He got his gun and fired some shots over their heads. The boys ran, but they yelled that they would get even with him. Those were the boys Dan saw the night of the fire."

"That's scary," said Liza. "Hank and Ted yelled the same thing at Hermit Dan."

"It sure scared us," said Widow Hawkins. "We had never locked anything here before, but for a long time after the fire we did. And that was when Dan changed. Day and night for several days he sifted through the rubble. He even slept by it. He didn't want anybody around. But he did ask us one favor."

"What was that?" asked Bill.

"He had to go over to Mainland for something," said Widow Hawkins. "He asked a couple of us to watch the place for him. We sat right by it. He came back with a big package. It seemed to be heavy, but he didn't open it. He thanked us and we went home. Then a few nights later, Dan left and was gone for years. Nobody heard a word from him. The police tried to find him. They had caught the two boys and wanted to tell him. But they couldn't find a trace of him. Then one day he came back. He built that shack and moved in. He was just the way he is today."

The children were quiet for a long while. Each was lost in his own thoughts about Hermit Dan.

Finally, Jed said, "But he did change before he left the island?"

"Yes," said Widow Hawkins.

"How awful it must have been for him to watch his dreams go up in smoke," said Liza.

Widow Hawkins looked at Liza. She said, "You know, I never thought about it in that way. Perhaps that is what happened."

"But it seems as if he would have gotten over it," said Bill.

"I guess some things you never get over," said Jed. "By the way, what is his last name?"

"Hampton," said Widow Hawkins. "He talks to me, but only about his garden and things in general. I make him a little birthday cake every year and leave it on his table. But he never mentions it. I just find the empty plate on my back porch."

"When is his birthday?" asked Liza.

"July fifteenth," said Widow Hawkins.

"Thanks for telling us all of this," said Jed. "Grandpa is talking to Captain Ned. We'll find some way to keep Hermit Dan from having anything else hurt him."

"So how about that lemonade and cookies now?" asked Widow Hawkins.

Suddenly they heard a loud yapping and scratching at the door.

"Jelly Bean," said the children.

"How did he find us?" asked Bill.

"He used his nose," said Widow Hawkins. She went and let him in. "I guess he wants some cookies, too. Does he like lemonade?"

"That crazy dog would probably eat dill pickles if you gave them to him."

"Come on in the kitchen," said Widow Hawkins. "Then it won't matter if he spills."

Soon the children and Jelly Bean were happily eating.

"I hope you'll give Gran this cookie recipe," said Bill. "I've never had any like this before."

"I guess not," said Widow Hawkins. "I made up the recipe."

"You did!" said Liza.

"Yes," said Widow Hawkins, "but I'll make sure Gran gets it."

"Thanks so much," said Jed. "We had better go now."

The children started home with Jelly Bean prancing around them.

"Oh, I forgot to ask her something," said Liza. She ran back to the house. Widow Hawkins was still on the porch. Liza said, "Captain Ned said Hermit Dan goes to Mainland once a month. Is it any special day?"

"The fifteenth," said Widow Hawkins. "He goes as regular as clockwork."

"Thanks," said Liza. She ran back to Jed and Bill.

13

A Scary Time

Gran, Grandpa and the children got back home at just the same time.

"How was your visit?" asked Gran.

"Great," said Bill. "She had the best cookies."

"And, Gran," said Liza, "she made up the recipe herself."

"Doesn't surprise me," said Gran. "She makes up most of her recipes."

"What did Captain Ned say?" asked Jed. "That's more important than cookies."

"He was as concerned as we are," said Grandpa. "He said he had heard about that family from the islanders. But the regular summer people were just trying to wait it out. The family will be here for just a few days longer.

They rented the house from some people who couldn't come until later. Ned didn't like it at all. But he said he would go down later this afternoon and talk to them."

"That's a relief," said Liza.

"Say," said Bill, "now that that's taken care of, why don't we go and get our softball team started?"

"But, Bill," said Liza, "you know what we planned."

Bill scratched his head and thought. Then he said, "Oh, yeah, but we can do that tonight, can't we?"

"Do what?" asked Grandpa.

"Oh, just a plan we had," said Jed. "Bill is right. It can wait. Okay, Liza?"

"Okay by me," said Liza.

Bill got the ball and bat. The children started toward the other end of the island.

"You almost blew it that time," said Jed.

"I don't see why," said Bill. "It can wait, can't it?"

"I guess so," said Jed. "Anyway, we can keep an eye on Hank and Ted down there. But if they start up this way, we follow."

"You bet we will," said Bill.

The summer children were glad to see them.

"Hooray, softball at last," said Paul.

"Unless Ted and Hank decide to take the ball," said Liza.

"Oh, we don't have to worry about them this afternoon," said Suzy. "They went to Mainland with their parents."

"And they're going to get me a new ball," said Marie. "Daddy was so mad when I showed him what they did that he went right over. The Holmeses screamed at Daddy, but he wouldn't leave until they promised to replace the ball."

"Good for him," said Bill. "Let's get started."

Soon the sides were chosen and the game began. They played for about an hour. Then Liza and Suzy sat down.

"I'm just too tired," said Suzy.

"And so am I," said Liza. "I'm going home and take a nap."

The others agreed they had played long enough. Bill and Jed were ready to go with Liza.

"But you don't have to lug that bat and ball if you don't want to," said Steve. "I'll be glad to keep it."

"Okay," said Jed. "We won't need it unless we're down here."

"I'll be careful with it," said Steve.

"We're not worried," said Jed. "Use it when you like."

Then the children started home. They were quiet. Even though they never liked to admit being tired, they all were. It seemed such a long way.

They were right in front of Hermit Dan's when it happened. The sky turned a strange color. It was eerie.

"I'm scared," said Liza. "I never saw the sky like that before."

"Something's going to happen," said Jed.

"Think we should try to get to the house?" asked Bill.

But none of them could move. The wind started. It whipped the sand into a whirlwind.

"A sandstorm!" shouted Liza. "What do we do?"

"Run to the nearest house," said Jed.

"But we can't," said Bill. "Hermit Dan's is the only house here."

The storm quickly grew worse. The sand was getting into their eyes and mouths. They were beginning to choke. They couldn't see. Never had the children been so frightened. They clung together, too afraid to move.

Then came a voice saying, "Catch my hand and hold on, you little idiots."

There was no mistaking Hermit Dan's voice. The children quickly obeyed him.

"Now run," said Hermit Dan. The children ran as fast as they could. But it was hard. They couldn't see and they were choking more and more. At last they were on Hermit Dan's porch.

"Get inside quick," he shouted. He opened the door and they slipped in. He tried to close it. But the wind was too strong. The children rushed to help him push. Finally the door was bolted.

"Didn't your grandfather tell you anything?" asked Hermit Dan.

"Yes, sir," said Jed. "He told us this might happen."

"Then why did you just stand there?" asked Hermit Dan.

"Because we were afraid," said Liza. "Grandpa said to go to the nearest house."

"But we were afraid of you," said Bill.

"That's stupid," said Hermit Dan. "Nobody would let his worst enemy die in a sandstorm. I may shout at you when you get in the way. But I'm not going to let anything happen to you."

"We're sorry," said Liza.

"Go in the back and get the sand out of your eyes," said Hermit Dan.

The children did as they were told. They were surprised to see that Hermit Dan did not have running water. An old-fashioned pump was at the sink. The water felt good and cold. It was a relief to wash the sand out of their eyes and mouths.

Liza looked around. She said, "This place is spotless."

"I kind of like it," said Bill. "Not a lot of clutter around. Just good simple living."

"It's the way the early settlers lived," said Liza. "Sure would make keeping house easier."

"Yeah," said Jed. "I wouldn't mind living this way myself."

"It has its advantages," said Hermit Dan. The children hadn't heard him come in. He went to the pump and started washing his own face. The children went back into the big room.

Soon Hermit Dan came in. He stirred up the fire in the fireplace. The children were glad. It had gotten cold.

Large iron kettles hung over the fire. An open-door oven was on one side. Hermit Dan looked into a kettle.

"I'll have to add a few things to the stew," he said. "I reckon you kids can hold pretty much."

"Can I help you?" asked Liza. Hermit Dan looked at her for a minute. Then he said, "No, no thank you. I know where everything is. It won't take long."

His voice was softer than they had ever heard it. The children looked at each other when he had gone.

"He may be our friend yet," said Bill.

"He already is," said Jed. "We could have died out there."

96

The children looked at the swirling sand. They had never seen anything like it before.

Hermit Dan came back and added things to his stew.

"A new experience for you, isn't it?" he asked.

"It sure is," said Bill.

"How long do these storms usually last?" asked Jed.

"They vary," said Hermit Dan. "Sometimes just a few hours, sometimes a day or so."

"Don't they let up at all?" asked Bill.

"Yes," said Hermit Dan. "There are lulls. That's one thing that makes them so dangerous. A lull will come and people think the storm is over and go out. Many a stranger has been killed that way."

"But how do you know when it's really over?" asked Liza.

"I'll know," said Hermit Dan. "In the meantime, you just settle in. I've got things to do."

Hermit Dan started to the back room. Then he turned and said, "There's a deck of cards on that shelf. It might help you to pass the time."

He went out of the room. The children looked after him in surprise. They were more puzzled by him than ever.

"Anybody for rummy?" asked Bill.

"Might as well," said Jed. "We seem to be stuck here for a while."

The children got involved in the game. Soon they were laughing. They had almost forgotten about the storm.

14

Raining Mud?

Hermit Dan went about getting supper ready. Every once in a while he would stop and look over at the children. But he said nothing to them. Suddenly Bill sniffed and said, "What is that scrumptious-smelling thing?"

"Sourdough bread," said Hermit Dan.

"I was having such a good time I forgot where I was," said Liza.

"Finish that game and then we can eat," said Hermit Dan.

The children threw down the cards.

"Who has to finish the game?" said Bill. "All you have to say is 'eat' and the game's over for me."

"I can't wait to taste that bread," said Liza.

"So the table's turned," said Bill. "You always say I'm the one who thinks of nothing but food."

Liza grinned and said, "Well, you do. But I like to try new things."

"You'll have to make do with tin plates," said Hermit Dan.

"We're used to that," said Jed.

"You are!" said Hermit Dan. "I never would have thought that."

"We go camping a lot," said Liza. "Mom says paper plates are too wasteful except for special occasions. So we use tin ones."

"A sensible woman," said Hermit Dan. He took the bread from the big fireplace oven and cut it into squares. He said, "Butter's over there."

The children each took a big square and put piles of butter on it. Then Hermit Dan dished up the stew.

"Man, you're some cook," said Bill, smacking his lips. "What's in this, anyway?"

Hermit Dan almost smiled as he said, "A little bit of just about everything."

"What kind of meat is this?" asked Jed. "I really like it."

"Rabbit," said Hermit Dan.

"I thought rabbits weren't in season," said Bill.

"They're not," said Hermit Dan. "This was a frozen one. I don't go much for these newfangled contraptions. But some of them come in handy. Jenny Hawkins has a freezer. That keeps us in meat."

"Don't you ever buy any?" asked Bill.

"No need to," said Hermit Dan. "Plenty of wild meat and fish around. And I raise enough chickens to give us a change."

"But what about beef?" said Liza. "Don't you like that?"

"Sure do," said Hermit Dan. "Would love to sink my teeth into a thick steak. But it costs too much."

"With this kind of cooking, I think I could do without beef myself," said Jed.

"I agree," said Liza.

The children settled down to eat in earnest. Hermit Dan kept looking out of the window at the storm. Then he said, "A lull is beginning. I expect your folks are worried about you. I'm going to get Jenny to call them."

"Gran and Grandpa!" said Liza. "I forgot about them."

"Don't you want me to go?" asked Jed.

"You three just stay put," said Hermit Dan gruffly. "I'll tend to this."

Hermit Dan sounded like his old self on that. The children didn't argue.

"Do you think he would mind if I had some more stew?" said Bill.

"See how much is in the pot," said Jed. "I think he wants us to eat a lot."

"There's a lot left," said Bill. "Anybody else want more?"

100

"I don't," said Liza. "But is there any of that bread left?"

"Plenty of it," said Bill. Liza and Jed both took another piece.

When they finished, Liza said, "I'm going to wash the dishes while he's gone."

"I don't know about that, Liza," said Bill. "He might not like it."

"I'm going to do it anyway," said Liza. "See if one of those pots has hot water in it."

It did. Jed took a thick cloth and carried the pot into the back room. Liza washed and the boys dried. In just a few minutes the place was spic and span again. They put more water in the pot and put it back where it had been.

The children began playing cards again. Jed happened to look out of the window.

"Oh, oh," he said. "The storm is starting again. I do wish Hermit Dan would hurry."

"Maybe he'll stay at Widow Hawkins's," said Bill.

"I doubt it," said Liza. Then a minute later she said, "You know, I was thinking. . . ."

Bill interrupted, "That's something new."

"I'm serious," said Liza. "I think we should stop saying Widow Hawkins and Hermit Dan."

"We don't do it to their faces," said Bill.

"I know," said Liza. "But we might forget and slip up. Let's start saying Mrs. Hawkins and Mr. Dan."

"Agreed," said Jed.

Just then the door opened. Hermit Dan came in. He seemed out of breath. The children rushed to help him close the door.

Then Liza threw her arms around him and said, "I'm so glad you're back. We were worried."

Hermit Dan didn't say anything, but neither did he push Liza away.

"Did you get Gran and Grandpa?" asked Bill.

"I asked Jenny to do it," said Hermit Dan. "I didn't

want to leave you all alone. I could see the storm was about to start again. But it will soon be over."

"How can you tell?" asked Jed.

"By the color of the sky," said Hermit Dan. "You'll soon see something you never saw before."

"Oh, what is it?" asked Liza. "Do tell us, Mr. Dan."

Hermit Dan looked at the children. He said, "Mr. Dan. It's been many a year since I've been called that." Then he shook his head, "No, I won't tell you. I'll let it be a surprise."

Then he noticed the dishes had been done. He said, "Your parents are bringing you up right. Are you ready for dessert?"

"Dessert!" said Bill. "I'm always ready for that."

Hermit Dan brought out a dish of raspberries covered with thick cream.

"You really know what we like," said Liza.

"I should," said Hermit Dan. "Caught you red-handed trying to raid my patch."

The children laughed. Bill said, "And we really caught it from you, too. We won't do that again."

"But we deserved it," said Jed. "Grandpa gave it to us, too."

"I figured he would if he found out," said Hermit Dan. He kept looking out of the window. Suddenly he said, "Now! Look out of the window now."

The children ran to the window. It was raining. But it wasn't like any rain the children had ever seen before.

"It's raining mud!" said Liza.

"How is it doing that?" asked Bill.

"The air is filled with sand," said Hermit Dan. "When you mix sand and water, what do you get?"

"Mud!" shouted the children. They kept their faces glued to the window. They didn't want to miss a minute of it. But it was soon over. Then something else happened.

"Look!" said Liza.

"A rainbow!" said Bill.

104

"I never saw one so bright," said Jed.

"Oh, it's so pretty it makes me want to cry," said Liza.

"Control yourself, twin sister," said Bill.

"All right," said Hermit Dan. "Out with you. It's safe now."

"Thank you for taking care of us," said Jed.

"Just the code of the island," said Hermit Dan gruffly. "Now get along with you."

The children quickly left.

15

Making Plans

The children walked home slowly. The rainbow was beginning to fade. Liza happened to look back. She stopped.

"Hey, fellows!" she called. They turned to see what she wanted. Liza just pointed. There was Hermit Dan working on his dunes.

"There has to be a secret there," said Jed.

"But how do we find out what it is?" asked Bill. "I'm not about to poke around those dunes again."

"But I'll bet Hank and Ted will," said Jed. "And it will have to be soon. They're leaving in a couple of days. We've just got to make plans."

"What's the date of today?" asked Liza.

"The date?" said Bill. "What does that have to do with this?"

"I was wondering if it was close to the fifteenth," said Liza.

"What's special about the fifteenth?" asked Bill.

"Oh, Bill, sometimes you can be so dumb," said Liza. "Don't you remember anything?"

"Not about the fifteenth," said Bill.

"I see what you're getting at," said Jed. "That just might tell us a lot."

"All right," said Bill. "So I'm dumb. Keep your old secrets."

Bill went running off. Liza started to call him, but Jed said, "Let him go. He'll cool down by the time we get home. What is your plan?"

"I thought we could sort of follow Mr. Dan and see what he does," said Liza. "I'm sure Gran and Granpa will let us go to Mainland. He always takes the first boat and we could, too. Then we'll come back when he does. When we get back, we can hide and spy on him. That way we can find out if his trips have anything to do with the dunes."

"You really have been thinking!" said Jed. "Do we just tell Gran and Grandpa we've decided we want to go to Mainland?"

"That would be the truth for me," said Liza. "I need to get some picture post cards. I promised I would write to some friends."

"But if we all go, Hank and Ted would have a free

hand," said Jed. "Maybe one of us had better stay and keep guard."

"I hadn't thought about that," said Liza. "Do you think we could get the summer kids to help?"

"I would rather not," said Jed. "It might get them in trouble. You know how scared they are of Hank and Ted. Maybe Bill can help. Sometimes he comes up with really good ideas."

A misty rain began to fall. Liza and Jed ran on to the house. Bill was in the kitchen telling Gran and Grandpa all that had happened.

"I thought you had gotten lost," said Grandpa.

"We were just talking," said Liza.

"Keeping secrets from me," said Bill. He was still angry.

"Ah, come on, Bill," said Jed. "We were just trying to figure something out."

"And you went stamping off before we had a chance," said Liza.

"Yeah, I bet," said Bill. He picked up the sugar bowl and started to throw it.

"Bill Roberts!" said Gran. "Don't you dare throw that."

"Just calm down, son," said Grandpa. "Remember what we talked about not too long ago."

Bill's face was red. He was getting angrier and angrier. But he put the bowl down. Then he stamped out of the house shouting, "None of you understand!"

In a few minutes, they heard a chopping noise.

Grandpa chuckled and said, "He's coming along."

"What do you mean?" asked Liza.

"Remember that last big fight he and Jed had?" asked Grandpa. "When we talked about it, I suggested he take out his anger by chopping wood. And he seems to be doing just that."

"Were you keeping secrets from him?" asked Gran.

"No," said Jed. "Liza had an idea and Bill didn't catch on to it."

"But I did call him dumb," said Liza. "Should I go apologize?"

"Not now," said Grandpa. "Do it when he cools off."

Liza and Jed talked with Gran and Grandpa about the storm and Hermit Dan.

"I can't say we weren't worried about you," said Grandpa. "We were afraid you had gotten caught in the strip between the summer houses and the islanders."

"It was such a relief when Jenny called," said Gran.

"We were scared there for a few minutes ourselves," said Jed.

"We sure were," said Liza. "We knew what we were supposed to do. But Mr. Dan's house was the only one near."

"Oh, it's Mr. Dan now," said Grandpa.

"And Mrs. Hawkins," said Jed. "It sounds better."

109

Just then the door burst open and in came Bill. He said, "Hey, Grandpa, it worked. I'm not one bit angry now."

"I figured it would," said Grandpa. "It worked with your father."

"Say, did you two ever find out what the date is?" asked Bill.

"Date?" said Liza and Jed together.

Then Bill howled with laughter. He said, "Now who's dumb?"

Suddenly everybody was laughing with Bill. Then Liza asked, "What is the date?"

"July fourteenth," said Gran. "Why?"

"Oh, nothing special," said Liza. "We were just wondering. The time is going so fast."

"Is it still raining, Bill?" asked Gran.

"Yes," said Bill. "Not a hard rain. Just a slow drizzle."

"The island needs it," said Grandpa. "Usually after a sandstorm it rains for the next day or so."

Liza and Jed looked at each other.

"Come on," said Jed. "Let's go to my room."

"We're going to play rummy," said Gran. "Would you like to join us?"

"No, thanks," said Bill. "We played enough of that for one day."

The children went to Jed's room.

"Boy, that was a relief when Grandpa said it would probably rain tonight and tomorrow," said Jed.

"It sure was," said Liza. "Now we don't have to worry about Hank and Ted. I hope it pours. They will think Mr. Dan is at home. I don't think they want to tangle with his stick again."

"And I did remember what the fifteenth meant," said Bill.

"Hooray," said Liza. "Now we've got to figure out other things, and we need your help."

"Right with you," said Bill. They filled Bill in on what the plans were so far. Then Jed said. "We've got to find a way to keep watch on his place until Hank and Ted leave. That's where we need your help."

"That's easy," said Bill. "During the day, we'll just go to the other end of the island. If they start up this way, so will we."

"But what about night?" asked Liza. "That's what worries me."

"We managed to go into the woods one night," said Bill. "I think we can sneak out for a couple of nights."

"Or we may not have to," said Jed. "You know what Gran said about the island."

"Yeah," said Bill. "It was the safest place ever and she wouldn't worry about us. But that was before Hank and Ted."

"But I don't think she would suspect they would try anything at night," said Jed.

"I don't, either," said Liza. "It's us we'll have trouble with."

111

"What do you mean?" asked Bill.

"Remember, we've tried this kind of thing before," said Liza. "But we always goofed because we couldn't stay awake."

"We'll use an alarm clock," said Bill. "We could take shifts that way."

"Now you're thinking," said Jed. "We'll camp on this side of the dunes. Mr. Dan won't even know we're there."

"You know," said Bill, "I think we're pretty smart."

Liza jumped up. The boys looked at her.

"Then again, I wonder if we're smart at all," she said.

"What goes with you?" asked Bill.

"I just remembered something else about the fifteenth," said Liza. Both boys looked puzzled.

"It's Mr. Dan's birthday!" said Liza.

"By gosh, you're right," said Jed. "So what do we do about that?"

The children thought about this for a long time. Then Bill said, "I know!"

He told Liza and Jed his idea.

"Hey, that's super," said Jed. "But do we have enough money?"

"Let's count up and see," said Liza. The children each got what money he or she had and counted. They added it up.

"Ten dollars," said Jed. "That should be enough."

"I've got another idea," said Bill. "You know Mrs. Hawkins said she always makes a birthday cake for him?"

112

"Yes," said Jed. "But how does that help?"

"A surprise party!" said Liza.

"That's right," said Bill.

But Jed shook his head and said, "I don't think we could ever get him over here."

"Oh, I don't know," said Bill. "We can find some way."

"How?" asked Liza.

"Think," said Bill. "This is important."

Soon Jed said, "I don't know whether this would work or not."

"What?" asked Liza and Bill.

"He did ask Grandpa to help him with that fence," said Jed. "Grandpa can ask him for help with something tomorrow night."

"Let's go talk to him," said Liza.

"Hold it," said Jed. "Hank and Ted are still a problem."

"That's a tough one," said Bill.

"It doesn't have to be," said Liza. "You know that whistle you have, Bill?"

"The one nobody will let me use?" asked Bill.

"Right," said Liza. "Do you have it with you?"

"Where I go, it goes," said Bill.

"Good," said Liza. "We'll take turns guarding during the party. That way we won't be missed. If anything happens, we just blow the whistle."

"And that settles that," said Bill. "I knew that whistle would come in handy."

"Now we can talk to Grandpa and Gran," said Jed.

"Gosh," said Liza. "We need to talk to Mrs. Hawkins and Captain Ned, too."

"First things first," said Jed.

The children raced down the stairs. Bill was yelling, "Gran, Grandpa!"

"What is it? What is it?" said Gran. "Has something happened?"

"Sorry," said Liza. "We're just excited."

Quickly the children told them their plans. Then Gran and Grandpa were excited, too.

114

"Another party," said Gran. "The islanders will love that."

"It's sure worth a try," said Grandpa. "After the way he took such good care of you today, it just might work."

"But you know Dan," said Gran. "Don't be too disappointed if it doesn't."

"Oh, we'll make it work," said Bill. "If he won't come here, we will take the party there."

Grandpa chuckled and said, "That would shake him up."

"And that may be just what he needs," said Gran.

"We'd better get over to Mrs. Hawkins's," said Bill.

"Why don't you call her?" said Grandpa. "You can't go running all over the island tonight."

"But we really need to see her," said Liza.

"Would you like me to call the others?" asked Gran.

"Would you, Gran?" said Jed. "It sure would help."

"Come on, boys, let's go," said Liza.

"I'll go, too," said Grandpa, "and talk to Dan."

The soft rain felt good as they walked across the sand. Even Jelly Bean seemed to enjoy it.

Mrs. Hawkins was as excited at the idea as Gran and Grandpa.

"You children certainly have livened up the island this summer," she said. "I'll make an extra-big cake."

She and the children decided how to decorate it.

When they got back to the house, Liza said, "Gran,

115

would you order our present? You know more about those things than we do."

"Certainly," said Gran.

"But remember, we pay for it," said Jed.

"What did Mr. Dan say?" asked Bill.

"Just to send word when I needed him. He would be glad to help," said Grandpa.

"Yippee!" shouted the children.

"All right, bedtime," said Gran.

The children thought they were too excited to sleep. But they were very tired. Sleep came quickly for them.

16

Three Spies

The next morning the children got up and dressed quickly in their best play clothes.

"My," said Gran, "you look nice."

"We're going on a trip," said Bill.

Grandpa chuckled and said, "I guess it is a trip. You haven't even asked about Mainland since you've been here."

"We've been too busy," said Jed. "Anything we can get for you, Gran?"

"Just some balloons," said Gran. "Nora says she has everything else. I didn't know it, but this is the kind of work she did at one time."

"She sure knows how to do it," said Bill.

"Yes," said Liza. "Our party was beautiful."

Grandpa looked at his watch and said, "Better eat breakfast if you plan to make the first boat."

"And you must wear your raincoats," said Gran. "It's raining hard."

"Ah, Gran," said Bill. "We don't mind a little rain."

"Gran has spoken," said Grandpa in a teasing voice.

"Oh, all right," said Bill. The three ate quickly, grabbed their raincoats and left.

Then they heard a "Yap, yap, yap" behind them.

"Oh, no!" said Liza. "Jelly Bean. We can't take him."

Bill scooped him up. He said, "You go on. The boat's there. I'll take Jelly Bean home. Try to get them to hold the boat for me."

Bill was off. Liza and Jed went onto the boat. They told the captain about Bill.

"He doesn't have to worry," said the Captain. "We've got five minutes yet."

Bill just made it. He said, "That dog!"

The children paid their fares and got on the boat. They looked for Hermit Dan. He sat right in front and looked straight ahead.

Jed whispered, "Keep quiet. Then he may not even see us."

Liza and Bill nodded.

It wasn't a long trip. The children had no trouble staying quiet. At Mainland, Hermit Dan was the first one off. The children checked to see when the next boat left. Then they followed him. He went straight to the post office window. The lady handed him a letter.

"That's strange," said Jed. "I wonder why he doesn't have his mail delivered on the boat like the others."

"He probably has his reasons," said Bill. "And we're going to find them out."

When Hermit Dan started out of the post office, the children started walking the other way. Then they turned to follow him.

"Now where?" said Liza. Hermit Dan walked so fast they had trouble keeping anywhere near. Then he turned into the bank. There were a lot of people there, so the children went in.

"Okay," said Jed. "You have a hood on your raincoat, Liza. See if you can get close enough to see what he does."

Liza put on her hood. She got as close as she could to the line Hermit Dan was in. While he was waiting, he opened his letter and took out a check. At the teller's window, he wrote his name on the back and handed it to the lady. She counted out some bills and gave them to him. Neither of them said a word. Liza turned away then. And Hermit Dan left the bank.

"Could you see how much he got?" asked Bill.

"No," said Liza. "It was only three bills, but I wasn't close enough to hear the teller count them."

"Come on," said Jed. "We don't want to lose him now."

The children were back on the street. They saw Hermit

Dan ahead of them. He went into the general store. The children followed him to the door. There were only three other people in the store.

"We'd better watch from here," said Jed. "He would be sure to spot us if we went in."

"But I've got to go in," said Liza. "I've got to get my cards and the balloons."

"Wait," said Jed. "He probably won't be in there long. Does everybody know where the dock is?"

"Sure," said Bill. "It's at the end of the main street. How could we miss it?"

"Okay," said Jed. "When he comes out you go in, Liza. Bill or I will follow him. We know when the next boat leaves. If we get too separated, we can meet at the dock."

"Do you want me to buy anything for you?" asked Liza.

"Yes," said Bill. "Five post cards. Get them of Pirate Island if they have any."

"I would like five, too," said Jed.

"All right," said Liza. "Gosh, I forgot. We need stamps, too."

"I'll go get the stamps," said Bill. "Jed can follow Hermit Dan. How many stamps do we need?"

Liza figured it up and said, "Twenty."

"You really mean to write, don't you?" said Bill.

"I promised," said Liza. "Do you have enough money?"

"Sure," said Bill.

Jed had been watching Hermit Dan.

"He's just buying groceries," he said.

"I didn't think he ever bought anything," said Liza.

"It's just coffee, sugar and stuff like that," said Jed. "Things he can't grow."

They saw Hermit Dan pay and pick up his bags. Quickly they ducked around the corner. But Hermit Dan didn't look right or left. He headed toward the dock.

"Okay," said Jed. "I'll follow him. We'll meet at the dock."

Liza went into the store. She looked at the wall clock and saw she had plenty of time. So she looked around the store before she bought her things. Then she took her time walking to the dock. When she got there, she saw neither Jed nor Bill. Liza got scared. Suppose the boat had left early. Would they have left her? Then she saw Hermit Dan sitting under the dock shed.

Thank goodness, she thought. Now I know the boys are around somewhere.

"Psst, Liza," whispered Bill. Liza turned. Bill stuck his head out from behind a barrel. Quickly Liza joined him.

"Where's Jed?" she whispered.

"Right here," said Jed from behind another barrel. "What took you so long? We were getting worried."

"I knew we had plenty of time," said Liza. "So I looked around the store. They have everything."

Just then the boat whistle sounded. This boat was larger than the one they had come over on.

"That clock you looked at must have been wrong," said Bill. "You really cut it close."

"That's just the warning whistle," said Jed. "The boat won't leave for another ten minutes. Let's wait and see where Mr. Dan goes."

They didn't have to wait long. As soon as the whistle had sounded, Hermit Dan took his packages and got on the boat. The children waited until they saw where he was going. He went right up front, just as he had coming over. So the children stayed in back.

"At least we can talk this trip," said Bill.

"Yes," said Jed. "We have to decide what to do when we get back."

"I thought we were just going to follow him," said Liza.

"Yeah," said Bill. "That's what I thought."

"But I remembered Gran's grocery order will be on this boat," said Jed. "Grandpa will be at the dock with the wagon. We'll have to help him."

"That does change things," said Bill. "Now what do we do?"

"I think I know," said Liza.

"Speak up, sister, speak up," said Bill.

"I can say I need to tell Mrs. Hawkins something," said Liza. "You two can help Grandpa and I'll follow Mr. Dan."

"So we get to do all the hard work, huh?" said Bill.

Liza flared up and said, "Then you say you have to speak to her. I don't mind helping with the groceries. But somebody has to follow Mr. Dan."

"I was just teasing," said Bill. "That's a good idea. Give me your package and I'll take it."

"But be careful, Liza," said Jed. "Don't let him see you."

"That won't be hard," said Liza.

"That red raincoat is awfully hard to miss," said Bill.

"Listen, you two," said Liza. "I've got some sense. He'll put his groceries away first. Right?"

"Probably," said Jed.

"That will give me time to hide behind that clump of bushes before you get to the dunes," said Liza. "I can see from there."

"The lady detective scores again," said Bill. "Sometimes you make me proud to be your twin. But just sometimes."

"That goes both ways," said Liza.

Soon the boat pulled into their island dock. Hermit Dan was the first one off. Sure enough, there was Grandpa with the wagon and no raincoat.

"Hey," said Bill, "it stopped raining. I didn't even notice."

The children were the last off the boat. Hermit Dan was already on his way home. Liza hurriedly explained to Grandpa what she had to do. He asked no questions. She gave Jed her raincoat and started running.

17

The Big Battle

Liza hurried because she wanted to be well hidden if Hermit Dan did come out to the dunes. And she was right to hurry. She had just gotten herself settled down when Hermit Dan's door opened. He came out and looked all around. Then he headed for the dunes. Liza was so excited she could hardly stay still.

Hermit Dan kneeled by the dunes and began to dig. Soon he pulled out a black box. Liza held her breath. She wanted so badly to see what was in it. But she couldn't. Hermit Dan reached in his pocket and pulled out two bills. He put them into the box and closed it. He put the box back in its place and covered it up. Liza watched as he replaced the reeds and grass. Then he stood up and went inside. Nobody would have ever known the dunes had been disturbed.

"Gosh," said Liza to herself, "we were right. The dunes do hold treasure. Where are those boys?"

She waited a few minutes longer. Then she went back to the house. Jed and Bill were just coming out.

"Why didn't you come?" asked Liza.

"Couldn't," said Bill. "Gran made us help put the groceries away and eat lunch."

"Did anything happen?" asked Jed.

"Did it ever!" said Liza. She told the boys everything she had seen.

"We really missed out on that one!" said Bill. "So what's the next step?"

"We just have to keep constant guard somehow," said Jed.

"Then we'll carry out the plans we made last night," said Bill.

"Get that whistle ready, Bill," said Liza. "We may need it during the party."

"It's right here," said Bill.

"We're not wanted around this afternoon," said Jed. "Nora likes to work alone. But Gran said for you to come in and get some lunch."

"I could sure use it," said Liza. "What are you going to do?"

"We'll go down to the other end of the island," said Jed. "We can keep watch there. Come on down after you eat."

The boys left and Liza went in for her lunch. Gran was

in the kitchen. She said, "There you are. I just put your lunch in the refrigerator."

Liza got her plate and began to eat. She said, "Is there anything I can do, Gran?"

"No, dear," said Gran. "Everything seems to be shaping up. Oh, Nora's calling me."

Gran left Liza to finish her lunch. Liza did this quickly. But she was curious as to what Nora was doing. She stopped by the dining room.

"Oooh," she said. "It looks like a fairyland."

"Do you really like it?" asked Nora. "I have such fun doing it."

"It's even prettier than ours was," said Liza. "And I didn't think anything could be."

Nora's face showed how pleased she was.

"I've got to go find the boys," said Liza.

"Have fun," said Gran. "But don't get too tired."

"We won't," said Liza.

"Yap, yap, yap." Liza looked down. Jelly Bean was looking up at her.

"Oh, all right," said Liza. "You can come, but it's a long walk."

The puppy happily bounced along after Liza.

Liza was in no hurry to get to the other end of the island. She knew the boys had everything under control. She decided to stop by Mrs. Hawkins's and look at the cake. She could see Mrs. Hawkins through the kitchen window. So she went to the back door.

"I couldn't wait to see the cake," said Liza.

"I just put the finishing touches on it," said Mrs. Hawkins. "How does it look?"

"Much too pretty to cut," said Liza.

She chatted with Mrs. Hawkins for a few minutes and said, "I've got to go now. The boys are waiting for me at the other end of the island."

Suddenly they heard voices outside.

"Stop!" shouted Hermit Dan. "Bring back that box!"

Liza and Mrs. Hawkins rushed out. Hermit Dan was waving his stick and chasing two boys.

"It's Hank and Ted!" said Liza. "Call the police. I've got to find Jed and Bill."

But Jed and Bill were there. They were already after the boys. Liza ran to Hermit Dan. She put her arms around him and said, "Don't worry. We'll catch them."

Hermit Dan didn't say a word. There were tears in his faded blue eyes.

Liza ran after the boys and Jelly Bean ran after Liza. Hank and Ted were fast runners. Bill and Jed were, too. But the older boys were almost at the other end of the island before they caught them. The other children heard the shouting and came running.

Jed tackled Hank. Hank dropped the box. Liza quickly grabbed it. Then Bill knocked Ted down. The four boys began to fight.

Liza saw that Jed and Bill were getting the worst of it. She handed the box to Suzy and said, "Hold this."

Suzy took the box and Liza jumped into the fight. Jelly Bean ran around in circles, yapping his heart out. When the others saw Liza, they went into action, too. Soon the two boys were pinned to the ground. Four held Hank. Four more held Ted. The others surrounded them. Both boys were screaming at the top of their lungs.

Liza picked up Jelly Bean and cuddled him. He was shaking all over. Liza turned to her brothers and asked, "Are you all right?"

"A little battle-scarred," said Bill.

"But nothing broken," said Jed. "'Those guys can really fight. Thanks for pitching in."

"And you, too, Jelly Bean," said Bill, patting him on the head.

"Where's the box?" asked Jed.

"Here it is," said Suzy. She gave it to him.

By that time, all the parents were there. They wanted to know what was going on. Before the children could explain, Mr. and Mrs. Holmes started in. Mrs. Holmes said, "Let my boys go. That's not fair, all of you ganging up on them."

"Let them go this instant," said Mr. Holmes.

"We can't do that," said Liza. "They are thieves. We have to wait for the police."

Jed and Bill looked at her. Liza said, "I told Mrs. Hawkins to call them."

130

"Good girl," said Jed.

"The police!" said Mrs. Holmes.

"We'll see about that," said Mr. Holmes. He started toward the children. But he was quickly stopped by the other men. Just then they heard the siren of the police boat. Captain Ned's boat pulled up at the same time.

18

Justice

"What's the trouble here?" asked a policeman.

All the children started to talk at once.

"Hold it," said the policeman. "Just one of you tell the story."

"Go ahead, Jed," said Captain Ned. "You tell it."

"Aren't you even going to let my boys get up?" said Mrs. Holmes.

The children looked at the policeman.

"I think you can let them go," said one.

The children let go. Hank and Ted got up. Ted immediately started to run. But a policeman grabbed him and said, "Hold it, boy."

"Better cuff them," said Captain Ned. "They're a mean lot."

"Oh, no," said Mrs. Holmes, "not my boys. They meant no harm."

The policemen looked at Captain Ned. They all knew him.

"Cuff them," said Captain Ned sternly. So Hank and Ted were soon cuffed together.

"Now let's hear your story," said the police chief.

The children told the story as quickly as they could. They even told about the boys popping Marie's ball. The policemen listened. One took notes.

"Now what do you boys have to say about all this?" said the chief.

"We didn't do anything wrong," said Hank. "That old man beat us for climbing his dunes. We were just getting even. Mom and Dad said we had to take up for ourselves."

"But didn't he ask you to leave?" asked the chief.

"He yelled at us," said Ted. "We don't let anybody yell at us."

"But you were on his property," said the chief.

"So what!" screamed Hank. "He's just a stupid old man."

Bill and Liza were about to explode. Jed whispered, "Hold on."

"What about the children here?" asked the chief. "What gave you the right to bully them?"

"We were just teasing," said Hank. "They're sissies. Can't even take a joke."

"Is popping someone else's new ball your idea of a joke?" asked the chief.

"So what's a little old ball?" said Ted.

"That's enough of this grilling," said Mr. Holmes. "I want a lawyer."

"Well, sir," said the chief. "You're going to need one. We have to take these boys into juvenile custody."

"What!" said Mrs. Holmes. "You're going to arrest our boys for a little thing like that?"

"Stealing is stealing," said the chief. "And they were caught red-handed."

Hank and Ted looked at Liza, Jed and Bill. Hank snarled, "We'll get even with you."

Captain Ned heard him. He said, "Oh, no, you won't."

Then he turned to their parents and said, "Start packing. You're leaving this island today."

"But you can't do that to us," said Mrs. Holmes. "We have our rights."

"Sorry, Mam," said the chief. "But Captain Ned runs this island. We'll oversee them, Captain. We can take them all to Mainland at the same time."

"Thank you," said Captain Ned. "I've got more important things to do."

Then he looked at Liza, Bill and Jed. He said, "That's a real shiner you have, Liza."

"I do?" said Liza. "No wonder it's hurting."

"Are you two all right?" he asked Bill and Jed.

"Couldn't be better," said Bill with a big grin.

"Want a lift back?" asked Captain Ned.

"Thank you," said Liza. "But we'll walk."

134

Jed turned to the police chief and asked, "Could we please go now? We've got to get this back to Mr. Dan."

"Just a minute, you three," said a woman. "I'm Suzy's mother, but I'm also a nurse. You come with me so I can clean you up."

The children didn't want to, but they went. Then they were glad they did.

"There now," she said. "You look a bit better."

"That medicine must be magic," said Liza. "My eye hardly hurts at all now."

"Thank you for fixing us up," said Jed. "But we've got to hurry now."

"We all thank you," said Marie's father. "Do come down often."

"We will," said Bill. "We've got to get our softball team organized."

That started everybody laughing and gave the children a chance to get away.

"Okay," said Liza. "Now tell me the part you didn't tell the police."

"We didn't feel easy going to the end of the island," said Jed. "We were afraid Hank and Ted might have had the same idea we did."

"So we decided to use your hiding place," said Bill. "Then when you came, we could check out this end of the island."

"But you didn't come." said Jed.

"I went by to see Mrs. Hawkins," said Liza.

"Well, it's lucky you did," said Bill.

"Hank and Ted were hiding farther down," said Jed. "They saw Mr. Dan leave his house. Then in a few minutes they headed for the dunes."

"How did Mr. Dan know?" asked Liza.

"I guess he forgot something," said Bill. "Anyway, he came back just in time to see the boys taking his box."

"And you know the rest," said Jed.

"Say, Liza," said Bill, "you're some fighter. And, boy, I needed help. But I never thought I'd see my sister with a black eye!"

"And that was quick thinking to call the police," said Jed. "Whoever says women can't be detectives should meet you."

Liza grinned. Then she said, "But I can't understand why the others didn't help before."

"Everything happened so fast," said Jed. "I don't think they knew what it was about until you gave Suzy the box. But when they pitched in, they sure pitched in."

They came in sight of Hermit Dan's house.

"Gee," said Bill. "I expected to see him still standing there."

"Mrs. Hawkins is probably with him," said Jed.

"I hope she didn't take him to her house," said Liza. "It would spoil everything if he saw the cake."

"Cake!" said Bill. "By gosh, I forgot all about the party. Do you think he will still come over?"

"Yes," said Jed. "I think he's a man of his word."

136

"But I wish all this hadn't happened," said Liza. "He was so upset."

"He'll be all right as soon as he sees his box," said Jed.

"Well, for pity's sake, let's stop poking along and get it to him," said Bill. The children ran toward Hermit Dan's shack.

Mrs. Hawkins heard them running and opened the door. Hermit Dan and Captain Ned were inside.

"Here it is, Mr. Dan," yelled Liza. "And not a bit worse for its little trip."

Hermit Dan took the box and clutched it to him. He was smiling.

"Ned told me the whole story," he said. "You three must have been regular little tigers to take on those boys. They're twice your size."

"Size doesn't always matter," said Bill. "We weren't going to let them do that to you."

"And the other kids pitched in and helped us," said Jed.

"It still looks as if you got a few battle scars," said Mrs. Hawkins. Then she noticed Liza and said, "Oh, Liza, your eye!"

"It's a real shiner," said Captain Ned.

"My first one!" said Liza with a big grin.

"My dear," said Hermit Dan. "It must feel awful."

"It did at first," said Liza. "But Suzy's mother is a nurse. She put something on it and I hardly feel it."

"She cleaned all of us up," said Bill.

"Thank goodness for that," said Mrs. Hawkins. "Your grandparents would have been horrified to see you all beat up."

Bill laughed and said, "Oh, they wouldn't be surprised. They're used to us."

"And now," said Liza, "your box can go back into its place in the dunes. I don't think anybody will bother it again."

"Oh, no, it won't," said Captain Ned. "Come on, Dan, we've got to hurry to get to the bank before it closes."

"All right, all right," said Hermit Dan. He looked at the children and said, "Suddenly everybody is ordering me around."

He said it with such a funny face that the children laughed.

"And it's high time, too," said Mrs. Hawkins. "It took these three children to wake us up."

The men started away. Liza called, "Don't forget Grandpa wants you tonight."

"Are you going to be a boss, too?" said Hermit Dan. "Life will never be the same."

He hurried after Captain Ned.

"What's that all about?" asked Bill.

"We don't know the whole story," said Mrs. Hawkins. "But that's the box Dan rescued from the fire. It must have things he treasures in it."

"It has money in it," said Bill. "Liza saw him put it there."

They told Mrs. Hawkins about their day.

"Good for you," said Mrs. Hawkins. "For some reason, neither Dan nor his family before him trusted banks. I expect a fortune in cash burned when the house did. But Ned was so angry when he came, he really lit into Dan. And Dan listened. Ned explained banking to him. They're going to the bank now and get Dan squared away properly."

"That box really has me curious," said Bill. "I wonder what all is in it?"

"That we may never know," said Mrs. Hawkins. "But I have a feeling we'll soon have our old Dan back."

"Do you think he'll tell us the stories he used to tell you all?" asked Bill.

"After today, I wouldn't be surprised at anything," said Mrs. Hawkins. "But you had better get home. You do have a party to give tonight. Would you mind taking the cake for me?"

"Be glad to," said Jed. The children got the cake and walked on home.

19

A Surprise
Bonus

The children went around to the back door. Gran saw them through the kitchen window.

"Good grief!" she said. "What happened to you? Have you been fighting?"

"We sure have!" said Bill.

"Who's been fighting?" asked Grandpa, coming into the kitchen. "Wow! That's some shiner you have, Liza."

"Yep," said Liza. "It's a dilly, isn't it?"

"For goodness sake, tell us what happened," said Gran. "None of you look angry."

"Angry?" said Bill. "We weren't fighting one another."

"Start at the beginning and tell us what you've been up to," said Grandpa. They all sat at the table and Jed started telling the story. Liza and Bill interrupted when Jed left out anything.

"That does beat all," said Gran. "It's certainly never dull with you three around."

"And you say Dan really smiled and listened to somebody?" said Grandpa.

"He sure did," said Liza. "He even said I was one of his bosses."

"Will miracles never cease!" said Gran.

"I can't wait," said Bill. "I hope he'll tell us those pirate stories. We still want to find proof this really was a pirate island."

"Don't push him too fast," said Gran.

"And now you, young lady," said Grandpa. "Does your eye hurt badly?"

"Not a bit," said Liza. "Suzy's mother put something on it. It hurt something awful before that."

Then Liza reached into her pocket and said, "This is the medicine. She said to put it on when the eye starts hurting again."

"How thoughtful of her," said Gran. "Do you know her name? I'll call and thank her."

"It's Jacobs," said Liza.

"I'll call her now," said Gran. "You all get cleaned up. We're going to have an early supper and it's just about ready."

The children left the kitchen.

"I've got an idea," said Liza. "Let's dress up for the party."

"Dress up!" said Bill. "In what?"

142

"You know Mom always makes us take a dress-up outfit wherever we go," said Jed. "And I think it's a good idea."

"It is," said Bill. "I just forgot we had any dress clothes."

"But, Liza," said Jed, "what about Mr. Dan? One of us has to get him."

"Think we could talk Grandpa into doing it?" asked Bill.

"I'm sure he would if we asked him," said Liza.

"But what can we use as an excuse?" asked Jed.

"The truth," said Liza. "That we're tired and want to rest."

"That sounds okay to me," said Bill. "We'd better get washed."

"Oh," said Liza. "We've got to wrap the birthday present, too."

"You and Gran can do that," said Jed. "I'm all thumbs when it comes to ribbons and such."

Supper was a quick one. Grandpa agreed to get Hermit Dan. Gran said she had everything ready to wrap the present.

"When are the people coming?" asked Jed.

"Not until around eight," said Gran. "I wanted to get everything out of the way so I could rest a bit."

"I'd like to take a hot bath and a nap," said Liza. "Grandpa, would you call me when you leave to get Mr. Dan?"

"That I'll do," said Grandpa. "I'll even set the clock for myself. I think we all need a rest."

Liza and Gran wrapped the present. Then they all went to their rooms.

It seemed no time at all before Grandpa was waking everybody. Gran had gotten up earlier. The people were already arriving. The children got into their good clothes.

"Gee," said Bill, "it feels funny to be dressed up."

"I kind of like it," said Liza. "Oh, wait a minute. I forgot to put my ribbon on."

The boys waited. They all wanted to go in together.

"Yap! Yap! Yap!"

"Jelly Bean," said Liza. "We forgot all about you."

"Don't you have an extra ribbon, Liza?" asked Jed. "After all, Jelly Bean was in on this, too."

"He sure was," said Bill. "He yapped us to success during that fight."

Liza looked through her drawer. She said, "There, I knew I had one somewhere. One of you hold Jelly Bean."

Bill picked him up and Liza quickly put a big bow around his neck. Jelly Bean seemed pleased with himself as he went into the living room with the children.

"Now look at that, would you?" said Nora. "You put us to shame, you look so nice. Even Jelly Bean is dressed up."

"I didn't know this was that kind of party," said Captain Ned. "I guess we all better go home and start again."

144

"I'm as surprised as you are," said Gran. But the children could tell she was pleased.

They heard the front door open. Grandpa and Hermit Dan were talking. As they got to the living room, everybody yelled, "Surprise!"

Hermit Dan stood there with his tool kit. Then he tried to make his voice sound gruff as he said, "I don't have to ask whose idea this was."

He put his tool kit down and said, "When are you Robertses going home anyway? These children and that mongrel seem to be everywhere I look."

Then he looked at Mrs. Hawkins and said, "Jenny, where's my cake? It wasn't on my table when I got home this morning."

The children slipped out of the room. They lit the candles and brought the cake in. Everybody started singing "Happy Birthday." They set the cake in front of Hermit Dan.

"Now blow them all out, old man," said Captain Ned.

But Hermit Dan didn't. He turned to Mrs. Hawkins and said, "That one in the middle is the one to grow on, isn't it, Jenny?"

"You know very well it is," said Mrs. Hawkins.

"Then I don't need the other ones," he said. He pinched the flames out. Then he took a big puff and blew out the one that was left.

"I guess it's time I forgot the other ones and just started growing," he said. Everybody shouted and clapped.

Bill was getting impatient. His nap had made him hungry. He said, "Would you please bring your cake into the dining room and cut it?"

"Cut it!" said Hermit Dan, "Who said anything about cutting it? It's my cake, isn't it? Do I have to share it with you scamps?"

"If you want any of that ice cream Grandpa churned, you do," said Bill.

"All right, all right," said Hermit Dan. "Let's go."

He stopped at the door of the dining room and stared. Then he said, "Now that's the prettiest thing I've seen in many a year. Who did that? I know it wasn't these three. They were too busy."

"My Nora," said Captain Ned proudly.

"You picked yourself a mighty fine wife, Ned," said Hermit Dan.

"Well, don't forget she's my wife," said Captain Ned. "And I intend to keep her."

Grandpa came in with the dishes of ice cream.

"For goodness sake," he said, "would you all sit down so we can eat?"

Everybody found a place and Hermit Dan finally cut his cake. Liza passed around the plates. But Hermit Dan didn't eat much. He looked as excited as a small boy.

The children looked at each other. Then they went and got their present.

Hermit Dan looked at the package and then at the children.

"Read the card," said Liza, hopping from one foot to the other.

"Read it aloud," said Grandpa. "I didn't know anything about a card."

Hermit Dan read,

> "Chase us, yell at us, we don't care,
> Swing your stick at us, we won't scare,
> Do what you like, but from our end,
> We love you, you're our friend.
>
> Your brats,
> Liza, Bill and Jed"

"They've really got your number, old man," said Captain Ned.

Hermit Dan carefully put the card in his pocket.

"Do hurry and open your present," said Bill. "Or I'll open it for you."

"Oh, no, you won't," said Hermit Dan. Quickly he tore off the paper. He opened the box. First he looked surprised. Then he roared with laughter.

"You brats don't miss a trick," he said. He held up the box and there was a huge steak. Everybody laughed. But not as much as Hermit Dan. He laughed until the tears rolled down his cheeks. Then he told the others what he had said during the sandstorm.

Finally things quieted down. Everybody went into the living room for coffee.

Hermit Dan said, "I hear you three have been trying to find out if my ancestors were pirates."

"We believe they were," said Jed. "We told Grandpa we would prove it before the summer was over."

"And we hear you tell really neat stories," said Bill. "Would you tell them to us?"

"Please, Mr. Dan," said Liza.

"Some rainy day," said Hermit Dan. "But you say you wanted to make a believer out of your grandfather this summer?"

"Yes, sir," said Jed.

"Well, one good turn deserves another," said Hermit Dan. "You helped me, so now I'll help you. Meant to do this, anyway."

He reached into his pocket and pulled out three coins. He showed them to the children and asked, "Do you know what these are?"

"Pieces of eight!" shouted the children.

"Right," said Hermit Dan. "They've been in the family since our pirate days. All of my stories were true."

He gave a coin to each child. Everyone gathered around to look at them. Excitement filled the room.

"But you can't give these away," said Liza. "They're valuable."

"Oh, I have some more," said Hermit Dan.

"Why, you old scoundrel," said Captain Ned. "Why didn't you show them to us? Then we would have believed you."

"I couldn't," said Hermit Dan. "My parents were ashamed of the fact that pirates were in our background. I couldn't even mention them in the house."

"Then how did you know all those stories?" asked Mrs. Hawkins.

"There were some old trunks in the attic. I went through them and found a diary. That's where my stories came from," said Hermit Dan. "And that diary is in the safe-deposit box at the bank now."

Mrs. Hawkins got up. She said, "I've had all I can take for one day. I'm dizzy with excitement."

Hermit Dan looked at his watch. He said, "It is late. I'll walk with you, Jenny."

Everybody decided it was time to go. Nora said, "I'll come over tomorrow and help clean up."

"Oh, we can do it," said Bill. "This party has been the greatest."

"I agree," said Hermit Dan. "And I thank you all, especially you three. And by the way, there's a mess of raspberries ripe if you want to help me pick them."

"Do we ever!" said Liza.

After all the guests left, the family was happy to have a chance to relax.

"You three did it again," said Grandpa. "You did get proof this was really a pirate's island."

"And they did a lot more than that," said Gran.

"I still want to know the rest of Mr. Dan's story," said Jed. "I've got a feeling he has a lot more to tell."

"I'm satisfied," said Bill. "Think of the stories we'll have to tell when we get home."

"I think Bill has the right idea," said Gran. "Perhaps it's better if Dan's past is left just as it is."

"I'm willing to leave it," said Liza. "I like him the way he is."

"I could use a rest from mystery-solving, too," said Jed. "But somehow things seem to keep happening."

MS READ-a-thon— a simple way to start youngsters reading

Boys and girls between 6 and 14 can join the MS READ-a-thon and help find a cure for Multiple Sclerosis by reading books. And they get two rewards — the enjoyment of reading, and the great feeling that comes from helping others.

Parents and educators: For complete information call your local MS chapter. Or mail the coupon below.

Kids can help, too!

- - - - - - - - - - - - - - - - - - -

Mail to:
National Multiple Sclerosis Society
205 East 42nd Street
New York, N.Y. 10017

I would like more information about the MS READ-a-thon and how it can work in my area.

MS
Mystery
Sleuth

Name _____
(please print)

Address_____

City_____ State_____ Zip_____

Organization_____

1—80